THE FIREWORK GIRLS

JORDYN WHITE

LARGE PRINT EDITION

Published by Velvet Pen Books
United States of America

www.jordynwhitebooks.com

ISBN 978-1-945261-43-5

Printed in the USA

Cover Design: Letitia Hasser | RBA Designs

Midnight Heat

Chapter 1

After a nine-month separation, my dearest girlfriends and I have been reunited for a mere twenty minutes when Sam already starts in on me.

"Okay girls, we have a mission," she says. "We're finding Chloe a date for the reception."

I roll my eyes.

Isabella's wedding is in exactly five days. Only Sam would think that's still plenty of time to find me a date. Never mind that the wedding has practically already started.

It's the Monday afternoon before the marriage actually takes place this Saturday. The guests have been arriving at the Rivers Paradise Resort in spurts all day long. It's the most luxurious resort in California, hands down, located on the central California coast in Swan Pointe. Hartman College (where we all met) is just an hour and a half inland. We made various excursions to Swan Pointe all through college and I actually moved here after I graduated. I was only here for a few months, but I used to see the Rivers Paradise Resort, perched up on the hill overlooking the ocean, every day on my way to work.

Isabella's family are the only ones I know who are rich enough to not only have the reception here—which is common enough I suppose—but to also host the wedding party, family, and several friends and their guests for a freaking week-long extravaganza of activity for their only daughter's wedding. I think some thirty people are here already.

I was the last of the four of us to arrive and joined the girls at one of the resort's restaurants. We're sitting on the patio, sharing a platter of bruschetta and the most delicious bowl of calamari I've ever had. It's a spicy mango mix and it's damned awesome.

So, like I said, the wedding is more or less underway. To the normal person, the task of finding a date for the reception would seem to be out.

But not Sam. Oh no. Unless I'm misjudging that glint in her eye, she's pretty damned determined to find me a date for Saturday.

By the way, when Sam says "date," she means "a guy to fuck." Just to be clear.

Of course, there is this one little fact. I would've had a date for the wedding if all had gone as planned. As a matter of fact, I would've been bringing my freaking husband to the wedding. But things have been sort of a disaster for me in the love department lately. Now it's Isabella, not me, who's going to be the first Firework Girl to get hitched.

That's what we called ourselves when we were still in college. The Firework Girls. Maybe I'll tell you the story behind the name some other time, or maybe it'll suffice to know it involved a box of illegal fireworks, the frat boys infamous for the most rowdy parties, and damn near getting ourselves suspended freshman year.

Allow me to introduce you.

By day, Ashley is a laid-back hippy at heart. She even has the long blonde hair that hangs past her waist, which she wears in a single braid almost all the time. By night, she's a brilliant pianist who knows how to capture any heart listening. Sometimes it does seem she has an alter ego because every time she's on stage I think, <u>I can't believe that's our Ashley.</u> We all graduated from Hartman College last year, but she stuck around to work on her Master's in Music. I think she's a genius.

Isabella is every bit the Greek goddess her name suggests. She's a gorgeous Mediterranean brown beauty, has long legs that won't quit, and possesses a sense of self I envy. She tends to shock men (and women) who don't know better with her sharp intellect. To look at her, you'd never guess she's working on her Master's in Microbiology at Harvard. People have a way of underestimating Isabella. It only figures she ended up snagging her professor. I guess the college boys just weren't up to snuff.

Sam is the Anti-Isabella. We've said as much to her face and she rewards us with a bold, brash laugh that makes us giggle. She's not quite five feet four inches, has short blonde hair with a mind of its own, and says exactly what she's thinking all the time.

No matter what.

This may be a weird thing to say, given that I'm only twenty-two myself, but Sam keeps me young. She's going to be one of those spunky old grannies who makes people say, "You're only as old as you feel."

All I can say is, Sam would be the one to insist on finding me a date.

"It's a little late for that," I say.

"Pshaw," Sam says, "I found a date."

"What? You've been back two whole weeks and you managed to land a date for the wedding?" After college, Sam moved to Portland for a job, but wasn't too happy there. Our friend Jack found her a good marketing job in the town of Rosebrook, where Hartman College is and where Jack still lives. Neither one of them are terribly far from campus. She moved back from Portland a couple weeks ago.

"With who?" Isabella asks.

"A little stud-monster I met last weekend." She grins and pops a calamari into her mouth.

"Wait," I say. "You met this guy only a week ago and he's coming to the wedding with you?"

"All five days of it. I drove down here on a mission. I figured I'd have a better shot at convincing someone if he was a local guy."

I have to admit this is impressive, even for Sam. She has a knack for luring guys in but this is a new record. I, on the other hand, have a knack for chasing guys away.

"I don't know what you do to these guys' cocks that they're so willing to follow you around anywhere you go," Isabella says.

"Find me a cucumber and I'll show you."

"You're shameless," Ashley says, polishing off the last of her bruschetta.

"The zip-line thing helped," Sam says. "Apparently he's always wanted to go on the supposedly famous zip line they have here. I'd never even heard of it."

Well, that makes sense. Who wouldn't be tempted by five days of everything the Rivers Paradise Resort has to offer? I've been looking forward to doing a little playing here myself. The zip line is top of my list.

"Are you going on the zip line?" I ask. Sam, for all her mastery over the male species, is terrified of heights.

"I said I would." She rolls her eyes. "It's part of the deal."

I raise my brows. Maybe Sam doesn't have as much power over this male as it first seemed if she had to resort to a deal like that. But it's still pretty impressive, plucking a date for a five-day wedding out of thin air.

"Now all we need to do is get you a date," she says.

"No thanks."

"Come on. It'll be easy. It's not like we're trying to find someone for the whole thing. Just someone to dance with at the reception. And get lucky with afterwards." She waggles her eyebrows. "We could go to the Perched Owl tonight for cocktails. It's my new lucky place."

I exchange glances with Isabella and Ashley. Ashley's wearing an evil grin. "Oh, Chloe already got lucky at the Perched Owl."

"Shut up, Ashley." I do not want to relive that night.

"What's this?" Sam asks.

7

"She met a guy. The night of her Not Wedding."

"Whoa! Whoa!" Sam says, raising her hands in the air. "Why am I just now hearing about this?"

"Because it's not a big deal," I lie. It was a big deal, but I am absolutely, definitely, not going to talk about it. Even now, nine freaking months later, I get an ache in my chest whenever I think of Grayson Piers.

"Just how lucky did she get?" Sam asks.

"Sooooo lucky," Isabella and Ashley say in unison, before busting out laughing. It's an old joke and tells Sam everything she needs to know.

She raises her eyebrows and looks at me with fresh appreciation. "Chloe Sullivan, I underestimated you. Do I get details or what?"

The details are coming back to me, as if I'd needed any encouragement. For months I've dreamt about Grayson's body. God help me, I'm getting worked up now just thinking about it. But we did more than connect physically.

It's remembering the way our souls seemed to wrap around one another, as cozy and delicious as a hot bath. That's what gets my heart aching.

"It was only one night."

One night. The night. The night of the perfect storm. Not only was it the Night of Grayson, it would've been the night of my wedding.

According to the invitations we sent out, anyway. All hundred and seventy-eight of them, on my side alone. Then just two days after graduation and three months before we were set to get married, my ex up and decided to be my ex, and I had to send out Anti-Invitations telling everyone, no, never mind, we're not really getting married. Just kidding!

It was hell. After spending three and a half years of my college career as Brad and Chloe, I was just Chloe. An official graduate with a dual degree in Nothing Much and No Idea What I'm Doing.

The August after graduation, the girls decided they needed to come hang with me for a weekend of shopping and beach-lounging, to help me forget about the fact that I would've been getting married that weekend in a stunning brocade gown (still hanging in my closet, waiting for alterations that will never come). Unfortunately, Sam's body betrayed her (and me) and she ended up missing the whole thing so she could lie in bed in Portland with a severe case of the flu.

The only good thing about Sam's absence was that I knew no one would try to hook me up with some random guy that night. Even though it had only been three months since the breakup, Sam would've been hunting for someone on my behalf. Sam says 'Sex cures everything' as if she's kidding, but I suspect she's not.

But in the months following my breakup with Brad, I'd come to realize something. Though I did love him, looking back I could see how I was always kind of on his periphery. Like this pretty little accessory hanging off his arm.

For the last few years we were together, any time we did something, it was always what he wanted. Not that he was domineering, exactly. I just sort of_went along with things. I wanted what he wanted. After a while I didn't even know what I wanted.

By the night of my Not Wedding, I had decided this was not his fault.

So that's why, in spite of dear Sam's texts from Portland insisting I get out there and get things on with a man (no commitment necessary), I was really thinking I needed to not.

Just, not.

On the night of my Not Wedding, the three of us sat in tall chairs around a table at the Perched Owl, drinking cocktails and laughing about nothing much in particular. Our weekend was just about at its end—Isabella had to fly clear back to Boston early the next day—but it had been a great weekend. Not depressing at all, like I'd been afraid it might be. In fact, my brain kept returning to the strangest part of the whole thing.

Three months after Brad dumped me for his chemistry lab partner (I kid you not), I didn't really miss him. I mean, I missed being held and having someone to talk to about every stupid thing that crossed my mind, and I missed sex.

I really, really missed sex. (In fact, I'll blame the whole evening that was about to unfold on that little detail, if you don't mind.)

But Brad?

I didn't miss him like I thought I should. It was pretty clear to me, by the night of my Not Wedding, that it was probably all for the best.

In the nine months that have passed since my Not Wedding night, it's even more clear. It was definitely for the best. Because if I'd really loved Brad the way I thought I did, I wouldn't be wondering if the biggest regret of my life would turn out to be what happened the morning after the Night of Grayson.

Chapter 2

The Night of Grayson

It all began right there in the Perched Owl, in the very first moment I saw him.

Which makes me wonder just how pathetic I am.

But it's true. I remember exactly how it all went down. Isabella leaned back in her chair, draped one long arm over the back and said, "Two hopefuls. Four o'clock."

We followed her gaze and saw there were indeed a couple of "hopefuls" heading our way. Two guys who, I had to admit, had every reason to be hopeful.

The one was tall and dark and would've been a perfect match for Isabella if she didn't already have a boyfriend—now her fiancé—so loyal he moved to fucking Boston just to be with her.

The other guy was more my type. Like, the heart-stopping type. As in, my heart actually stopped when I looked at him and I literally don't know if that's ever happened to me.

He was wearing a dark, button-down shirt that made his chest look perfectly touchable and edible, and oh my god those broad shoulders. Am I the only girl that really notices the shoulders? I remember thinking that I could be perfectly happy hanging on to those babies in a moment of passion. (I was not wrong.)

I'm not usually so bold as to check out a guy's package (something Sam once told me she does not understand), but I didn't fail to notice his, wrapped up ever so nicely in his dark jeans thankyouverymuch. But when I looked back to his face, I couldn't pull my eyes away from his.

A stunning, slate blue. Dark blue, not like my icy blue eyes. They were gorgeous.

He and Mr. Greek God came right to our table. While I could say I didn't know who these guys came to see, it'd be a lie. Mr.

14

Greek God was zeroing in on Isabella (poor guy), and Blue Eyes was looking right at me.

Even then, I knew that look he was giving me was more than just a look. God, it started so quickly with Grayson. It's insane.

The noise of the crowd fell away and I damn near forgot my girlfriends were there with me. I took in his dark, brown hair, the subtle hint of curl on top, the neat stubble along his jawline. And those eyes. A little voice way in the back of my head was telling me I was <u>not interested, not interested, not interested</u>. But the rest of me was captured.

"Evening ladies." This from Mr. Greek God. He even had an accent and, we soon found out, a foreign-sounding name I've since forgotten. He introduced himself and shook our hands in turn before saying, "And this is Grayson."

Grayson shook our hands too, but he didn't go around the table in order the way his friend did. Though I was in the middle, he shook my hand last.

That was the first time I ever touched Grayson Piers. When he took my hand a jolt of electricity raced up my arm and got my heart sprinting.

He held my hand a bit longer than the others, just long enough to understand he wanted me to know he was there.

Did I ever.

When he finally released me, I tucked a lock of my auburn hair behind my ear with slightly trembling fingers.

Mere seconds passed when Isabella gracefully mentioned her devoted boyfriend and Ashley not-so-gracefully mentioned that, sorry boys, we're heading to the back patio for "a top-secret mission to mark the occasion of Chloe's Not Wedding Night."

This statement allowed me to, at last, pull my eyes from Grayson's so I could stare at Ashley with mortification.

The boys tactfully dismissed themselves, moving on to more fruitful pastures no doubt, and the girls and I were left to our own devices. And that was the end of Grayson.

Or so I thought.

The girls and I did, in fact, retreat to the patio only to decide it was too crowded and we should wait a bit longer. My first thought was, why <u>not</u> have a drink with Grayson and Mr. Greek God? Instead we found a table by the patio's beehive fireplace and talked for another hour or so. I told myself it was all for the best, even though I didn't really believe it.

Even now I try to tell myself it would've been better if I'd never seen him again.

I can't bring myself to believe that either.

Our "top-secret mission" was smashing champagne glasses (engraved with <u>Brad and Chloe Forever</u> and the fateful date) in the fireplace, once the back patio cleared away. It was an experience both thrilling and anti-climactic, if that makes any sense. Then we called it a night and headed back to my apartment.

It had been a full weekend, and Ashley and Isabella had to get up early the next morning. The first leg of Isabella's flight back to Boston was so early, she insisted we say our goodbyes that night. She and Ashley would let themselves out in the morning, and Ashley would drop her off at the airport on her way back to Hartman.

I agreed to this plan to satisfy them, but still intended to get out of bed long enough to say goodbye anyway. Who knew how long it would be before we'd see each other again?

We'd been home from the Perched Owl only ten minutes when I realized I forgot my bag on the patio. I don't usually carry a bag when I go out like that. I prefer to tuck my keys, my cards, and my phone in a pocket and leave it at that. But because of the sacrificial champagne glasses, I'd needed a bag. At one point in the evening, I'd dropped my phone in there.

I didn't realize my error until I went to charge my phone for the night. The other two were in the bathrooms changing, so I knocked on one door, told Ashley where I was going, and headed back.

Fifteen minutes later, as I walked up to the entrance of the Perched Owl, there were Grayson and Mr. Greek God, waving their goodbyes to each other. His friend walked off, but Grayson stood still, having noticed me.

I managed to keep walking. My skin began to tingle all over, as if my body knew before I did what was coming.

"Ah, you came back for me," he said, teasing. He gave me a crooked smile. That was the first time I noticed his dimple. Just one. On his left cheek.

"I left my bag on the patio," I said, still walking, "and when I find it I'm going to tuck you inside and smuggle you out."

Don't ask what possessed me to make such a flirty comment.

"In that case," he held open the door for me, "I'd better help you look."

Grayson fell into step behind me as we made our way through the main bar and toward the double doors leading to the back patio. I felt his eyes on me the whole way.

There was a cluster of guys around one of the patio tables and I quickened my step, wondering if they'd seen (and perhaps taken) my bag. I went through the doors and glanced at the table nearest the fireplace, where the girls and I had spent the last part of our evening. The black strap of my bag hung from the back of the chair I'd been sitting in and I exhaled in relief.

"I see it." I hurried toward it. I was acutely aware of Grayson's presence as I grabbed my bag and did a quick check of the interior.

"Everything there?"

It was mainly the empty box that had held the glasses, but there was my phone, right next to it. I nodded and looked up at him. He was giving me a most delicious-looking grin. "Ah, well. I'm happy for you and everything, but how am I going to be able to talk to you now that my Knight-in-Shining Armor strategy didn't pan out?"

"You already had a rescue strategy?" I smiled back. It was a flirty smile. I'll admit it.

"A guy's gotta be quick on his feet if he wants to capture the attention of a beautiful woman. Maybe I can join your spy ring instead."

"My what?"

"Aren't you ladies spies? What with your top-secret mission and everything."

How Grayson managed to pull off mentioning that without embarrassing the hell out of me, I don't know. He was just so easy-going and... I don't know, accepting. I didn't feel the slightest bit awkward. In fact, I felt inclined to play along.

"Well, only the best of the best can be admitted to the Firework Spy Network."

"Oooh." His eyes lit up. "You even have a name for it."

"And now that you know our top-secret name, you definitely need to pass the spy test or, I'm very sorry to tell you, I'll have to dispose of you."

His grin turned devilish then, as if he couldn't imagine anything more pleasant than being tested by me. I grew pretty tingly myself.

As I said, I'll just blame it on his sex appeal and my sex-deprived state.

My phone dinged and I pulled it out of my bag.

Ashley: <u>Well?</u>

Me: Got it. Thanks.

I dropped my phone in my bag. "Sorry. My friend just wanted to make sure I found it."

"So what <u>was</u> the mission?"

I explained what we'd done with the glasses, gesturing toward the beehive fireplace. He nodded with approval and headed over, leaning in to inspect the ashes.

"I think we got all the pieces out," I said, watching him. My heart had been beating at an elevated rate ever since I'd seen him out front. Being free to take in his profile at my leisure only made things worse. Grayson Piers is impossibly handsome.

He straightened and looked at me. "Much more creative than burning photos." He grinned. "Did that get him out of your system?"

I shrugged. "I don't know that he's really been lingering in my system, to be honest. Does that seem strange?"

His smile broadened as he considered me. "No. I'd say that makes it your good fortune you weren't stuck with him for life. Maybe it was my good fortune, too, or I wouldn't be standing here talking to you."

I smiled and wondered if he found it as unusual as I did that we were talking about my Almost Husband so easily, and that it didn't lessen the draw I felt between us at all.

It is strange, right? But it didn't feel that way at the time.

I'm not sure how we managed to advance things from there, but we ended up settling on the wide stone hearth that wrapped around the front of the beehive fireplace. After a half hour of talking and tossing those first little flirtations at one another, I received another text from Ashley that read: <u>You okay?</u>

I glanced at him, sitting next to me looking intolerably sexy. I still hadn't gotten used to his looks. Actually, I don't know that I ever did. "Sorry. My friends are wondering about me."

"Roommates?"

"No, they're just in for the weekend. They leave at o'dark thirty in the morning though. I figured they'd be asleep by now. Hang on. It'll take just a second."

"Take your time." He gave me that delicious crooked smile. Yeah. I didn't plan on leaving any time soon.

Me: Just talking to someone. Don't wait up.

Ashley: Say WHAT? Who are you talking to?

Me: No one. Just someone. I'll fill you in later. Get to sleep. Seriously.

I silenced my phone and turned back to Grayson. Our conversation picked back up easily._When I mentioned I'd just graduated from Hartman College with a degree in Business Management he tilted his head and smiled.

"Really? You don't strike me as a Business Management kind of girl."

"I don't?" I tried not to look too pleased. "How do you see me?"

A slow smile spread across his face and I felt my cheeks get warm. I got warm in other places too, and let me tell you, I don't know that I've ever quite felt all <u>that</u> for a guy I'd just met. So quickly. So willingly. As fast as things happened with us, I suspect it still could've happened much sooner.

"I don't know," he answered, still smiling, "but something that doesn't involve a cubicle."

I was, in fact, working in a cubicle. I'd tried camouflaging its prison-gray panels with a few decorations, but it still felt like a damned cubicle.

"If you could do anything," he leaned closer, ratcheting up the electricity in the space between us, "what would it be?"

Have my way with you until you beg for mercy?

That should've been my first warning I was getting in too deep, because I <u>definitely</u> never thought anything like that about someone I hardly knew. Hell, I don't think I'd ever thought that about <u>anyone</u>. But Grayson. <u>Grayson.</u> He hooked me in every way a man can.

I managed to keep my cool, and ended up answering his 'If you could do anything' question more honestly than I'd planned. "Write a wildly successful food blog and make six figures a year doing it."

His eyebrows raised and I tried to not look mortified. I wasn't sure why I said it. True, I'd mentioned it to Brad a couple of times, but we both agreed it was a highly-unlikely scenario.

Brad said it would be better to apply my natural head for business and my organizational skills on a more sensible path. You know, degree. Job. Career. It had all made sense at the time.

And it worked. I did have a good job. At that shipping company in south Swan Pointe, I was making more than any of the Firework Girls (not including Isabella's trust fund), and fresh out of college. How could I argue with such a good starting salary, especially knowing I'd probably be making twice that amount in a few more years?

But I did want to argue with it. I did. I didn't realize just how strong that desire was until I confessed my nearly-forgotten dream to this dreamy stranger.

Just when I thought his raised brows indicated the same disdain Brad had for the idea, Grayson said, "Well that'd be a hell of a lot more interesting, wouldn't it? Just think, if you were famous, people would pay you to eat the food in their restaurants and you could write your reviews right there on your tablet."

He nodded as if he approved of the idea more and more. He smiled in such a way I wondered if I needed to hang on to something to keep from kissing him right then. I was losing control of myself a bit, but with a smile like that, he really wasn't playing fair.

In the middle of all that, I did not fail to notice <u>what</u> he was smiling at. My idea. My ridiculous, head-in-the-clouds idea. I found him more desirable for that reason alone.

"Yes, that sounds more like a Chloe thing to do."

I smiled and shrugged, trying not to reveal just how much I really would love to follow my silly dream. "Well, we all have our little fantasies. How many people actually make money blogging about food? A tiny minority. It's such a shot in the dark."

"Like YouTubers."

"Exactly."

He held his hand in the air for a minute. "Sorry, I should've been more clear. That's me. I'm a YouTuber."

"You're a... huh?"

He dropped his hand, still smiling.

"Sorry," I said, caught off guard. "I didn't mean to insult you."

He furrowed his brows and laughed. What is it about hearing a person really laugh for the first time that feels so exhilarating and intimate? Like you're seeing the first glimpse of the real them.

"How did you insult me?"

"Well, you know. The whole struggling to make it to the top of the heap thing." I'd read about how hard it is to make it to the top as a blogger. I knew vlogging was no different.

"Actually," he said easily, "it's how I make my living."

I blinked at him. He was still smiling. He didn't look like he was kidding.

I mean, I knew people did this. I knew. But... I'd never met one in person before and... well, I guess never knowing a real live successful YouTuber made it all seem like a pipe dream.

It was. Wasn't it?

I leaned in a little closer, my auburn hair sliding over my shoulder. "Really?"

"Is that so strange?" He laughed again. I smiled. I liked his laugh and wanted more of it, but suddenly I was zoomed in on the topic at hand.

"You really make a living doing that?" Even I could hear the desire in my own voice.

"Pretty cool, yeah? It's a lot of work and it took us a while to get it off the ground."

"Us?"

"Me and my friend Tom. We're both photographers and started filming how-to videos a couple years ago. Just kind of screwing around. About a year into it we were starting to see some income from ads and decided to go full broke. It took off like crazy a few months after that. Shuttersky Studios. Ever heard of us?"

I shake my head. "Where do you film? What'd you do to market your channel? Do you guys have jobs too or just this?"

"Whoa, one question at a time." He laughed again, looking completely yummy.

If Sam were here she'd say 'completely fuckable.' She'd be completely right.

But my attention was divided. I had a million questions. For one shining moment it seemed as if my dream wasn't so crazy after all, but it was only for a moment. I realized everyone's definition of 'making a living' was different. For all I knew he and Tom were splitting rent on a crappy apartment somewhere and living off beans and rice.

"We have a studio at Tom's house. Lights, backgrounds, a couple cameras. The whole works. But we've started spotlighting other photographers, so sometimes we travel to their studios or shoot outdoors instead."

Don't ask me why, but the topic was starting to make me feel uneasy. Scared, maybe. It was too much. This man was living a variation of my own dream. Dreams don't come true like that for people like me. They just don't. People like me get to cancel their Almost Weddings, work in cubicles, and spend their paychecks on mortgages they can't afford and Very Sensible Retirement Funds.

Maybe it was boring. Maybe so. But sometimes you have to be sensible. Being sensible helped me take care of myself and my brother when there was (almost) no one else to do it. I didn't have the luxury of risky dreams.

I remember very clearly thinking those things in that moment, while Grayson sat across from me talking about an interview they just did with some photographer from Sweden.

I enjoyed his story, but steered the conversation in other directions.

Not that that saved me. No matter what we talked about (our next in-depth topic was fucking global warming, if you can believe that) it was revealing. We were revealing. The sexual draw between us increased as the evening wore on, but so too did the sense that I'd known him forever already and could talk to him about anything.

I even told him about my most mortifying moment in high school. He'd laughed and put his arm around me and made me feel like it was the sort of thing that can happen to anyone. We were sitting close then—his hand on my thigh and my fingers absently playing with the hem of his shirt. He told me about a particularly memorable family holiday gathering when he was a child. I did pity him being the youngest of so many siblings and the target of their malice.

As he talked, part of me thought it was strange the way we were sitting. As if we were lovers already. But it felt so natural.

When he finished with his story, we looked at one another and didn't say a word for what seemed like forever. It was strangely comfortable, and so intimate for a man I'd just met. Then we kissed the most delectable kiss. I honestly don't know who leaned in first.

It was tender and almost sweet, the way he softly pressed his lips to mine.

We pulled away slowly, but stayed close as we looked into each other's eyes. He gave me a soft smile, which I returned.

He gently took my hand and we intertwined our fingers.

"I really love," he said softly, "how your nose piercing matches your eyes."

I have a little stud piercing, just above my left nostril, with an azure stone.

"Makes me want to kiss it," he said quietly.

My smile widened slightly. I liked the idea of him kissing it.

"Just like..." He leaned in, asking.

I tilted my head, granting permission.

He came in and gently placed his lips on the piercing, "...that." Then he planted a soft kiss on my lips.

He pulled away slightly. We hovered there, close together, and I felt like we were in our own little cocoon apart from the world.

I gave him a crooked smile. "I have a matching one in my belly button."

I had to laugh at his reaction. He looked like a little kid who'd just been promised a giant candy bar.

"Want to see it?"

"Uh, <u>yeah.</u>"

I smiled and gently untangled my hand from his. I pulled the sheer fabric of my top up to reveal the stud in my navel. It's bigger than the one in my nose, but the same color.

Not taking his eyes off it, Grayson slowly reached toward it. My skin tingled as his fingertips brushed over my belly button and the piercing.

His eyes darted up to mine. Looking at me then, his fingers brushed my belly button again. My breath shallowed and my whole body went alight.

I leaned toward him slightly.

His hand flattened out as it gently slid over my stomach and around to my side. We leaned into one another. I dropped the fabric of my shirt as we kissed again, his hand still on my bare stomach.

This time we lingered, opening to one another. That first time I tasted Grayson Piers, my insides trembled. As our tongues gently played together, I wrapped my arm around his waist, feeling his firm back for the first time. Our chests pressed lightly against one another.

I don't know how long we kissed, taking each other slowly, exploring, tasting. It was almost timid, that first lingering kiss with Grayson, but I felt wrapped in a plume of heat, quietly wanting him. But that kiss... it was sweet and perfect and makes my heart sigh remembering.

After we finally broke apart, we continued to talk. We sat with the top of my high-heeled foot pressed against the underside of his leg, his hand on my hip, my breasts touching his chest.

Before long, the evening took a definite turn. I don't remember much of what we talked about from there. Nothing much, I think. This and that. I do remember we discussed our mutual love for the chocolatier downtown, but only because our comments about the pleasures of sucking on their truffles were thinly-veiled teases about something else entirely.

We kissed again, more than once. Each time, our kisses were a little more urgent and our hands roamed a little more.

By the time he invited me back to his place, I was barely able to keep my cool. Inside I was burning so hot I hardly knew what to do with myself. I was too wrapped up in Grayson to regret that I'd never felt anything like that for Brad or anyone. I was in uncharted territory, that's for sure.

I followed Grayson's Mustang in my little Jetta, through the downtown area of Swan Pointe, and eventually up into the residential neighborhoods in the hills.

I remember once thinking, <u>I can't believe I'm doing this.</u> But I kept going.

Chapter 3

We pulled up to a gorgeous two-story house on Sinamone Street. I wondered if he had roommates or lived with his parents or something. I didn't know anyone our age with a house like that. It's on one of the more desirable ridges in town, with a magnificent view of the city—which glittered with lights—and the ocean beyond.

I pulled into the drive as he turned off his car and waited for me. Taking my hand, we entered the house through the garage. He flipped on the lights to the kitchen, which opened onto the dining and living areas. The far wall was lined with huge windows, presenting a view of the city lights. The soaring ceilings were accented with broad, wooden beams.

"Wow," I breathed as he set his keys on the counter and headed for the fridge. "I can only imagine the rent on this place."

A tactless thing to say, I know, but I couldn't seem to help myself around Grayson. It was like there weren't any boundaries between us.

He didn't seem bothered. "I'm not renting. I own it."

"Ah. Well, that's good." I drifted toward large kitchen island. "A mortgage payment would be less than rent, I would think."

"I wouldn't know," he said distractedly, opening the fridge. "I bought it outright." My stomach dropped to the floor. "Oh, good." He pulled out a couple beers. "I thought I was out. Want one?"

"Um..."

He owns this place <u>outright?</u> That couldn't be from YouTubing though. Right? Maybe he's a trust fund kid like Isabella.

He was staring at me, wearing that shirt that stretched just perfectly across his pecs.

A sexy, sexy trust fund brat.

Or... maybe he was as successful at YouTubing as he said. I knew such things were possible. You know, in theory. But being five feet from someone who's doing it made the whole thing seem more... real.

Within reach.

I was dying to ask him if he paid for his house with his earnings but I wouldn't go that far. I'd said more than I should already.

"Or...." he said, seemingly trying to decipher my expression. "I may have a wine cooler in the fridge in the garage? That's about it in terms of alcohol. I'm not as stocked as the bar, sorry." But he smiled. "Or I have water? Tea? Coffee? There's probably a can of pineapple juice in here somewhere." Holding the two beers in one hand, he held the refrigerator door open with the other and leaned down, apparently looking for said can of pineapple juice.

I regained my composure and circled the kitchen island. I was being stupid about his financial situation, whatever it was. It wasn't important and none of my business. Anyway, I figured I should focus on more important things. Like those sexy goddamn abs.

I drew close as he straightened up. I took one of the beers from his hand. My fingers brushed his and the jolt from touching him again raced up my arm and into my chest. I hadn't cooled much during the drive. If anything the opposite had occurred, and I was really just trying not to completely launch myself at him. "This is great. Thank you."

He looked at me, holding my gaze. If I'd had any doubts about his desire for me, I didn't have any doubts then. The refrigerator door was still open and I realized we were letting the cold air out. I barely felt it though, I was getting so hot. We both knew why I was there and my body was ready to go. In fact, I was slick with wanting him.

I think I said something about needing a bottle opener, but I'm not sure.

His eyes never left mine. He set his bottle on the island, took mine from my hand, positioned it at an angle next to the counter's edge, and popped off the cap with one swift tap.

Holding my eyes with a penetrating gaze, he held it out to me. I pursed my lips slightly and gave it a sideways glance, but didn't take it.

He moved ever so slightly nearer. Inches away. My eyes travelled over his chest, lingering, then came up to meet his gaze.

"You wanted something different?" he asked.

He wasn't asking about the drink any longer. He wasn't smiling any longer either. He looked ready to gobble me up. Oh, how I wanted him to.

I placed my hand on his muscular forearm, my heart pounding so hard I wondered if he could hear it. "I could go for something different."

As his hand circled my waist, my hand slid up the bare skin of his arm. I ran my other hand up his firm chest as our mouths came together, lips slightly apart. When his tongue slid into my mouth it was like lightening. I pressed myself against him. He kicked the refrigerator door closed and set my bottle on the counter with a thud before tightening his embrace.

As our tongues eagerly took each other, his hands moved down to my ass. I pressed my body against him in response, encouraging him. Our tongues worked together, his hands squeezing my rear and coming around to my breasts. My hands roamed freely as well, over his chest and back and tight ass. I surprised myself when I reached around to the front and found his sizeable bulge, squeezing it.

He massaged me even more eagerly. I found the button on his jeans, but struggled to unhook it because our bodies were pressed so tightly against each other.

He broke our kiss as if coming up for air. I got a glimpse of his smoldering eyes before he backed up enough to release the button and unzip his fly himself. I saw his hard cock straining against the black fabric of his briefs, but only for a moment.

He swiftly lifted me onto the counter and I exhaled in surprise. No one had ever set me on a counter like that, and let me tell you, it was fucking hot. He took one of my ample breasts into his hand, bent over and took it into his mouth right through my sheer top.

Exhaling heavily, I wanted his mouth on my bare skin. I leaned back, pulled off my top, and tossed it aside. He leaned down toward my belly button and kissed it before swirling his tongue around the stud. His hands were flat on my back and moving up toward my bra clasp. In seconds my lacy, turquoise bra was sailing through the air as well.

When he moved up and took my hard nipple into his warm mouth, I groaned and shuddered. God, it had been so long that my skin was super sensitive everywhere. Even so, I'd never been on the receiving end of someone who seemed so <u>hungry</u> for me. He was driving me mad.

All of a sudden, I was impatient for him to enter me. His tongue flicked back and forth over my nipple and I boldly wrapped my legs around his waist, unable to hide my wanting. One arm held me tight against him while his free hand massaged my other breast. I was going mad with what he was doing with his tongue. He sucked and pulled and ran his tongue all over my nipple. Every flick and pull resonated in my core and I squeezed him tighter against me.

My other breast ached for equal treatment and, as if he knew, he launched onto that one and sucked it so well I couldn't help but moan and grind against him shamelessly.

I was cursing my damn jeans and that damn counter. We didn't line up quite right and I was longing to feel his hard cock against my clit.

"Grayson—"

He came up and pressed his mouth hard against me. I opened to him and pressed hard back, wanting every part of him.

I fumbled for the button on my jeans but he pushed my hand away. "I want to do it," he said, his voice deep and husky. He unzipped me and I leaned back on my hands, lifting my hips slightly as he slid my jeans off and let them drop to the floor.

He took in my underwear—the lacey pair that went with my bra—and gave me a ravenous look. I was positively burning. I lifted my hips again and he slid off my underwear, but before I knew where it disappeared to, he bent over and dove between my legs. He took me into his mouth, his rough tongue sliding up my clit, and I cried out, arching my back and grabbing the hair on the back of his head. "Oh god!"

My entire body lit up as his tongue stroked me over and over again. His hands gripped my hips and held me close as I angled even more toward his hungry mouth. I was scandalizing myself, but there was no stopping then, not that I wanted to. In mere seconds I was dangerously close to going over the edge right there on his kitchen island, but I didn't want to. I didn't want it to be over so soon and I longed to have him inside me. But the waves of pleasure his tongue gave me were so intense I couldn't make him stop either.

Then it was too late.

My climax took me hard and fast and I arched back, doing my best to stifle my cries. Ripples of pleasure tore through my body again and again as he continued to work me. I curled forward as my orgasm reached a high I'd never known before.

I grabbed his broad shoulders as my body reached its last, delicious peak. But though I felt the satisfaction of an orgasm, my body didn't relax and cool as it usually did. I looked down and saw his tongue flicking on my clit, and I began rising again. Wanting him inside me still.

I pulled on his shoulders slightly, letting him know I wanted him to come up to me. He instantly took the hint and lifted me off the counter, carrying me. I wrapped my arms and legs around him. I was pressed against his bare chest, but still not aligned over his cock as I desperately wanted to be.

Feeling unleashed, I hungrily sucked on his neck and the back of his ear. When he groaned, the sound of his voice reverberated over my body. He didn't take me to a bedroom, as I expected. Instead we went into the darkened living room and he set me on the lounge.

I leaned all the way back, perfectly exposed, as he straightened up. He pulled a wallet from his back pocket, extracted a condom in gold foil, and held the corner of the packet between his teeth so he could finish undressing. I marveled that he made even this look sexy.

He pulled his jeans and briefs down to the floor in one smooth motion. His hard cock was so erect it was nearly flush against his pelvis. I sprung up at the sight of it and shocked myself even further by grabbing the base before he could do anything else. Scooting to the edge of my seat, I took his warm shaft into my mouth.

He groaned and grabbed the hair on the back of my head. "Oh, Chloe." My name on his lips sounded so good, I was determined to hear it again. I slid his shaft deep into my mouth, then sucked on it as I slowly drew it out. I finished by teasing the cleft at the head of his cock with my tongue. He groaned again, rewarding me with a "God, Chloe."

I'd done my share of fellatio in my time but I felt possessed in a way that was new to me. As I dove deep again, feeling his hardness strain even more, I sensed I was enjoying it as much as he was. Driven by instincts I didn't know I had, I fucked his cock until I was so wet and throbbing I almost couldn't stand it. "I want you," he said huskily.

I went down on him faster and harder, enjoying his groans, then pulled away and leaned back on the lounge. He tore open the package and slid the condom over his shaft with one smooth stroke. He came down on top of me and I hooked my heels around his thighs. His cock teased my opening.

Again, that voice in my head: <u>I can't believe I'm doing this.</u>

But it wasn't only shock at my own boldness, though it was that. It was wonder. At him.

Our eyes met and my heart was pounding as he looked right into me. My heart was aching for him as much as my body was. He did not deny me.

As his cock slid inside me at last, we gasped together. He plunged his tongue into my mouth as he dove deep inside me. Our mouths broke apart as I curled around him, my nose against his neck as his cock thrust into me over and over again. I was so hot and wet I was already nearing another orgasm. He hardened further and I spread myself wider, wrapping my arms around his shoulders.

We kissed again, his mouth firm against me as he let his full weight press on me. I reached both hands toward his tight ass as he worked me into a frenzy. My entire body pulsed with pleasure and I tightened around his cock as I climbed higher and higher.

I arched my head back and he sucked on my neck, groaning. He grew harder still and changed the angle he was coming at me. Suddenly he hit a tender spot inside me and I exploded with pleasure. Stunned, I cried out as he hit it again. And again. Intense pleasure rippled outward from that spot and I squeezed him tighter than a vise. In three and a half years with Brad, it was never like this.

He sent me careening over the edge in an orgasm that topped even the last one. Forceful waves wracked my body and my blood rushed through my ears. As I thrashed helplessly beneath him, his thrusts grew faster and more intense until at last he moaned loudly in my ear. He thrust into me sporadically and forcefully as we came together.

After what seemed an impossibly long time, my orgasm finally released me and began to subside. His movements within me began to slow. More gentle waves of pleasure washed over me and I sank back into the couch. Still tingling, I angled my hips, wanting him to press against me, which he did, firmly. He tucked his head down and his hot breaths warmed the crook of my neck. We pressed against each other, the last bits of pleasure anchoring into my body.

He pulled up onto his elbow, looked me deep in the eye, and thrust into me suddenly and hard. I arched my head back and closed my eyes as his thrust sent a tingling wave of sensation all over my body.

"God, Grayson," I whispered.

He put his mouth on mine before I even opened my eyes. I kept them closed as I sank into the depths of his kiss. He placed one warm hand on my cheek.

He pulled away but stayed close, and we looked at one another. I was captured, once again, by his stunning blue eyes.

He placed a soft kiss on the tip of my nose. He curved around and placed another kiss on my nose piercing.

He slowly reached up and kissed my forehead. He was still cradling my cheek so I felt wrapped in him, with his warm lips on my skin. I inhaled deeply through my nose, taking in his smell.

He moved to the side of my face and put a kiss on my temple. He lingered there, pressing gently, and I closed my eyes.

My heart was fluttering. It was the most intimate moment we'd shared yet.

He settled on his elbow and smiled at me. I felt strangely exhilarated and cozy.

"So," he lightly stroked my jaw with his thumb. "No to the beer, then?"

That was how it started. In the bar. In his kitchen. On his couch. Not too much later, on his couch again. I was impressed with his stamina, but if you want to know the truth, I was even more impressed with mine. I'd never been ready again so quickly. Never. I knew plenty of other women who could have sex over and over again on the same night but I'd never been one of them. I'd never physically wanted to.

I'd kind of wondered if maybe something was wrong with me. But that was the first time I'd considered that maybe it never had been me at all, because I couldn't get enough of Grayson that night.

For the first time, I could apply the word <u>passionate</u> to something I was experiencing. I couldn't help but wonder why it'd never been that way before, with anyone else.

As amazing as the sex was, if that night had only been about passion and sex, maybe things would've been different.

Maybe I wouldn't be hurting so much for him now.

Chapter 4

"So our little Chloe had a one-night stand," Sam says now. "Maybe she doesn't need my help getting a date. We can take her back to the Perched Owl and she'll nab one all by herself."

I need to change the subject. I know when Sam's focused about something and she's got this one set in her head. But no way. No. Fucking. Way. "I kind of have a date anyway."

"Who?"

"Bobby."

"Okay, number one," Sam rolls her eyes and holds up one finger, "he's only coming for the zip lining thing, so that doesn't count for the reception. Two," she lifts the second finger, "even if he _were_ coming to the reception, he still doesn't count because I'm pretty sure you're not getting lucky with your baby brother."

"Uck! God, Sam! I hope not."

"Stop harassing her," Isabella says. "By the way, Chloe, I got him his own room."

"Why? Everyone else is in one room." I know better than to say two rooms would be a waste of money. Isabella would just laugh and, given how much her family's spending on the wedding, she'd be right to. Still, I never take her abundance of money for granted, like it's somehow mine to claim.

"You didn't want to share a room with your brother did you?" Ashley pipes in.

As if I've never done that before. "It wouldn't have been a big deal. It's just a couple nights."

"Yeah, but what if you hook up with someone?" Sam asks.

"Will you lay off?"

"Not until you're laid, honey. You need it too, I can tell. You're all tense. Come on. A screaming orgasm never hurt anyone."

"It's a wedding and you're a hot bridesmaid." Isabella winks. "You never know."

54

"You're all hopeless."

"What if Bobby wants to hook up with someone?" Ashley asks sweetly.

I glare at her. "Stop talking right now."

Ashley laughs. They've all accused me of being overprotective of Bobby before. I admit, I spent a fair bit of energy my senior year making sure <u>he</u> didn't spend his freshman year swimming in a vat of beer at the frat house. But in those first years after our mom died, I was the only one looking out for him. Old habits die hard.

"Hold up," Sam says to me. "Give me one shot. I say we go to the Perched Owl after dinner tonight and find you a hot guy to be your date at the reception. I promise I'll find you someone completely fuckable. If not, you can trail after little Bobby tomorrow and worry <u>he's</u> going to find someone completely fuckable."

"<u>Anyway,</u>" I say pointedly, "tell me what happened with your Portland job. I never got to hear the story."

She gives me a look that tells me she's not done, but says, "Well, there's not a ton to tell." She's apparently had her fun for now and is going to let it go. Thank god. The last thing I need is another one night stand.

"It was a little disappointing because I wasn't working on anything exciting. Brochures and web copy and crap like that. That's to be expected when you're the newbie, I guess. The part that drove me crazy was my department head." She rolls her eyes and takes a sip of her beer. "Everything had to go through him and, let me tell you, that guy was an ass and a half. If I didn't need the job and a good reference I would've told him to stick it a week in."

"He didn't like your work?" Isabella asks.

Sam shrugs. "He liked it fine and knew how to make it better. He knows his shit, I'll give him that. I did learn a lot, but gawd he's just such an abrasive ass. Normally I like abrasive."

All three of us nod.

"But he had these pet names for everyone in the department, and that just irritated the hell out of me. He thinks he's being cute, but he's not and everyone just kind of tolerates it."

"How'd a guy like that end up in charge?" Isabella asks.

"What was his pet name for you?" I want to know.

Sam makes a face at me. "Munchkin. He even sang the fucking munchkin song to me once. The asshole."

I grin as she looks at Isabella. "Because his cousin is one of the partners, and because he's a damned designing genius. I hate that guy."

Isabella and I laugh. Maybe Sam looks upset, but trust me, when Sam's upset there's no question about it. No jokes. No calling anyone a genius. When she's pissed she's a little flaming ball of napalm and everyone with half a brain knows to get the hell out of her way.

She spends a few more minutes entertaining us with tales of her old job and filling us in on her new one, then we start talking about Isabella and Shane's honeymoon plans.

"How long are you going to be in Greece?" I ask.

"A couple weeks, but we actually just added a week to our trip so we can go to England too. He thinks we're just doing the London thing, but I have a surprise for him. I hired a researcher to look into his family history and she finally sent me what she found. She traced one of his lines all the way back to 1684 in Cornwall, England! His family even has a crest. So I'm taking him to check out the little village his family is from."

"Oh my god," Sam says, grinning, "you guys are such nerds."

Isabella sticks her tongue out. "I'm getting his crest framed for his office too. He's going to be so excited."

"Oh yeah," Sam says, leering, "how excited?"

"Shut up, Sam," Isabella retorts, but her smile says it all.

Sam laughs, then her eyes light on me suddenly. "Oh, Chloe! I was digging through your archives the other day and found your Turtle Brownie recipe." Her eyes roll up and she puts her hand on her chest. "Oh my God, soooooo good!"

I smile. "You liked them, huh?"

"Jack ate nearly the whole pan all by himself when I was at work one day."

"Is Jack still coming over and swiping your food?" Isabella asks.

"Some things never change." Ashley grins. True that. Our friend Jack has been swiping our food for <u>years.</u>

"I had to make another pan and hide it from him," Sam continues. "He found it eventually anyway but there were a couple left so I packed them. Yum, yum, yum, girl."

I smile and the conversation takes another random turn, the way conversations with your girlfriends tend to do. I have to admit though, I'm having difficulty paying attention. Because even Sam trying my Turtle Brownie recipe has its origin in Grayson Piers.

There's no escaping this man today.

Chapter 5

The Origin of Turtle Brownies

I asked for a tour of his house, but we didn't make it very far. Around the corner from the living area was a more casual room with a couch, TV, closet for pool supplies and towels, and a patio door leading to the outside. I made a comment about christening the couch, but we took each other so eagerly we ended up on the floor instead.

Afterward, we sat together, finally making it to the couch. I was still nude but all wrapped up in the soft throw he kept on the back of it. He sat next to me with just a portion of the blanket thrown over his lap, but his chest was still uncovered for me to enjoy.

We got to talking about his YouTube channel and how he and his friend Tom got the whole thing off the ground. It all sounded so perfect, I was surprised to hear him say he was ready to try something new.

"Don't you like it?"

"Yeah," he said simply, "it's fun and it's performing really great. But it's kind of... lost its novelty I guess. I enjoy photography but I'm more of a hobbyist. Tom's a professional and really passionate about it. He's been the driving force in some ways. I like what we're doing, but I think I want a new topic. Maybe something I could do on my own. I've been kicking around a few ideas."

"Like what?"

He shrugged. "I'm not sure yet. I'm leaning toward a travel channel."

"Now that would be fun."

He nodded and his eyes lit up. "Wouldn't it? I'm still trying to work out an angle though. It's really hard to get something that broad to take off."

"I once read a blog about this Canadian couple that picked up and moved to Columbia or somewhere. They started a blog and are making a living at it. I was so jealous.

Their blog is all about how to go be an expat somewhere. It was really interesting."

"Exactly. I need some way to narrow things down." He put his arm on the back of the couch and started lightly playing with my hair. "I'm tossing around some ideas. I'm kind of waiting for inspiration to strike. I know what it takes to get a channel going and I don't want to dive into something new unless I'm sure it's something that will keep me engaged for a while. I get bored kind of easily."

"Me too."

That's when I decided to fess up about my Job Application Addiction. "You know, this place where I work, it's a good company. The people are really nice. They're dedicated to their employees and try to promote from within. They've invested a lot of training in me already and my manager said that when one of their project managers leaves, they might move me into her position. She's quitting after she has her baby, but that's not for another five months. Anyway, it would just be a first step but it would at least put my degree to more use. I'd be supervising a few people and get a raise. But honestly? I don't want to do any of it. I mean, I'm sure I will. Why wouldn't I? But that doesn't stop me from putting out applications everywhere."

"Like where?"

"Really random crap all over the place. I don't know why I'm applying to any of these places, because aside from some of them not really being in my field, some are from out of state. I just feel so restless. It's like I'll hear about a city and start looking at job boards and before I know it, I'm applying for things. One day I looked up most livable cities or something and started going to their job boards. San Francisco. Chicago. Tallahassee. Tucson."

"I got my degree at U of A," he said. "Tucson's a great town."

I nodded. "That's what I hear. But I'm telling you, I've applied everywhere. Denver. Houston. Boise."

Little did I know that I'd be offered a job and on my way to Boise in less than a week.

"What's worse," I continued, "is that I've even had a few call backs but I never follow up. I mean, I can't just pick up and move to freaking Houston or wherever. Then the next week I'm right back at it again. I'm starting to feel like an addict."

He laughed.

"The thing is, I'm either applying to weird shit that I have <u>zero</u> qualifications for. Or I apply for stuff I might be qualified to do in five years or something. Or I apply to stuff I <u>am</u> qualified to do, because I just want to go... I don't know, <u>somewhere.</u> And of course, those are the people calling me back, but do I really want to pick up and move and spend all that money to haul my ass to Denver just to have another job that's going to bore the shit out of me?"

He laughed and nodded.

"Plus, my brother's here and I feel like I need to stay close."

"He's in Swan Pointe?" Grayson asked.

"No. Right now he's home with my dad, but in a couple weeks he'll be back at Hartman College. He's starting his sophomore year there."

"And where's home?"

"Temecula. It's between LA and San Diego. More inland though."

"So why do you feel you need to stay close to your brother? Is he your only one?"

I nod. "He's four years younger than me. Our mom died about eight years ago. He was just eleven, poor kid."

"Poor you, too," he said quietly, giving me a look of empathy (thank God it wasn't that pitying look I hate so much).

"Yeah, it was really hard."

He removed his arm from the back of the couch and took my hand. "How did she die? Can I ask?"

"Yeah, it's okay. She was driving home from work in the dead of winter. She hit a patch of black ice and her car flipped and went down into a ravine."

"I'm sorry," he said quietly.

"Yeah. Me too. I think about her every day. She was amazing," I smiled the smile I reserve for memories about my mom. "I think you would've liked her."

He smiled too.

"My dad really fell apart when it happened though. I mean, really bad. He'd get himself to work but that was about it. He's doing a lot better now, but for a few years there, I was kind of the mom and looking out for Bobby and trying to keep him together. He went off the deep end too and was failing all his classes. I mean all his classes. It was crazy. The principal would leave messages on the machine at the house and I don't even know what my dad did about it. Nothing that I could tell. So it kind of fell to me. I cooked and cleaned the house and threatened Bobby until he'd finally get some homework done and dad just sat on the couch like a zombie."

"Wow," he said softly.

I shrugged. It was what it was. "It's a lot better now. My English teacher stopped me after class one day. I think this was a year and a half after Mom died. I don't know how my teacher caught on to things but she asked me some questions and I told her just a little. She told me about this support group for kids who've lost a parent, but she thought it'd help all of us. I don't know, something about the way she described it really clicked with me. I spent three days harassing my dad about it and wouldn't let up. I finally told him he'd better take us or I was going to steal the car and run away."

Grayson raised his eyebrows and smiled, apparently impressed.

"I don't think I would've really done that, but I wasn't going to give up either. He finally signed us up and that first meeting was really good. They have activities for the kids to do while the adults go off and talk about whatever. I don't even remember what our first activity was. Maybe it was decorating the memory stones. I forget. Anyway, that group was good because we weren't, like, sitting around talking about everything and crying or something. It was a lot of fun and just... I don't know... just nice to be with other kids who knew what it was like, because most kids have no idea, you know?"

He nodded and squeezed my hand. I realized he was listening, really listening to me. I'd told Brad about my mom, of course, but I never really got into all this with him. I don't know why. I think he would've listened. He wasn't <u>that </u>much of an ass.

But... Grayson felt safer. I didn't quite realize how guarded I'd become with Brad until I sat there talking to Grayson about my mom and my family. And it felt okay.

"They had this anger activity once. I think this was our third meeting or something. Anyway, at the beginning the leaders talked about all the emotions you have after a parent dies, and how they're sometimes on the inside where no one can see them. I think they went through all the emotions, but that night they focused on anger. So everything was healthy ways to get it out, like popping bubble wrap. And we got to throw bean bags at a wall and try to knock off all these sticky notes. It was really fun and we really got into it. I remember watching Bobby as he was throwing those bean bags. He was laughing like the other kids, but I could see it in his eyes, you know? All the stuff underneath. The parents came back then because we had one last activity we were going to do with everyone, the parents too. It was this little race with wadded up balls of paper and hockey sticks."

Grayson was listening intently, stroking the back of my hand with his thumb.

"Anyway, so we did all this stuff and the leaders wrapped things up and I remember thinking how strange and refreshing it was to have someone acknowledge everything I was going through without me feeling like a pariah about it. It just was, and it was really nice. Then, I'll never forget this, on the way home, Dad said, 'I sure miss your mother.' And he didn't ever say stuff like that. He just didn't. I said 'Me too,' and then it was quiet for a while. I looked into the backseat and Bobby was crying pretty hard. A long time later he told me he'd never cried about her before. Can you imagine? This was like <u>two years</u> later and he finally cried over her. No wonder he was having such a hard time. Anyway, my dad noticed and reached back and patted Bobby's knee and then we were all crying and cried all the way home."

My eyes were watering just talking about it.

"It was really good though, you know?" I said, and Grayson nodded. "Things slowly got better after that."

I settled back against the couch cushions, done with my story. Grayson took a deep breath. "Well. It sounds like you saved your family there, Chloe."

I shrugged. I didn't know about that.

"It must be hard to let go of that responsibility, now that the crisis is over."

I laughed lightly. "The crisis is hardly over. My brother's in college mingling with frat boys." I rolled my eyes. "Me and my friends tried to keep a pretty close eye on him last year."

Grayson smiled. "Did he get into a lot of trouble?"

I sighed. "Not really, I guess. Normal stuff, really. But, you know, he's my baby brother. I don't want to see him get hurt."

"I can understand that." But he gave me a knowing smile, as if he knew better.

"I know. I need to let go." I'd known this for a while, but saying and doing were two different things sometimes.

"So, if you really, really <u>could</u> do anything. No restrictions. No barriers. No baby brothers to mother. If you could live any dream you wanted..."

I shrugged helplessly. "Still the food blog thing. Not a little one either. I'd want it to be huge. National. I'd have tons of great recipes, like my Turtle Brownies."

"Mmmm, that's sounds good."

"They're fucking amazing," I said, and he laughed. "But I'd also want to do reviews of local restaurants. I think it'd be fun. I love food. And not just the snobby stuff either. There's this place in Rosebrook just a block from my college. Delsa's Diner. They serve a concoction they call Volcano Fries."

I stopped long enough to make yummy sounds. He laughed.

"There's nothing upscale about those fries at <u>all</u>, but they're soooo good. I think it'd be fun to have reviews of places like that right alongside reviews of The Net."

He nodded. "Yeah, and you could do profiles of the owners or chefs or something. Then when your posts go live they'll tell everyone they know to check it out and that'll help drive traffic to your site."

"Good idea!"

"So why aren't you doing it?"

"Well..."

I didn't know the answer to that. I'd never talked with anyone who thought blogging could be a viable career path. I knew people did it, but like Brad always said...

I stopped my train of thought, wondering why that asshole was still up in my head. Everything with him was about being practical. Maybe I didn't want to be practical anymore.

Still, even with Grayson sitting right in front of me and making anything seem possible, I discovered letting go of old fears was not so easily done.

"Statistically, only a small number of bloggers actually make a living."

He shrugged. "What difference does that make? You know how many YouTubers aren't making money? Why should that stop me from doing it?"

I blinked at him. "Just... the odds?"

He shrugged again. "It's good to know what you're up against, sure. That's part of knowing what you have to do to succeed. But I enjoy what we're doing enough that I'm willing to put in the work required to beat the odds. And it is work. And it's hard. And we've had all kinds of setbacks we've had to get through. There were times I wondered if we were crazy for doing it. But I just kept thinking, this is what I want to do, so I'm doing it. It's no different than the guy who works his tail off in law school, right? I'm not afraid of work. I just want to spend it doing something I actually enjoy. Is that so crazy?"

"It sounds amazing. Like a fantasy."

He furrowed his brows at me and cocked his head, as if he sensed both my deep desire for this and my fear of even trying. Then he leaned in and asked the question that started to change everything.

Chapter 6

"Come on, Chloe. What's the worst that could happen?"

It wasn't a casual question. It was serious, and I knew it. We were getting to the heart of things now.

"Just," I said quietly, "I don't know. I guess that I'd put all that work in and nothing would happen. In the end I'd be right back where I started."

"Because it's not making money?"

"Well..." I shrugged, "yeah." But that suddenly wasn't feeling like a very good reason.

"If you try and fail," he said firmly, but gently, "that's <u>not</u> going back to where you are right now. Where you are right now, you're <u>always</u> going to wonder. You're always going to <u>wish</u>." He gave my hand a little squeeze and held my eyes. "It's always going to be a regret."

I felt that in my heart. How awful it sounded, too, to just always be wishing and hoping and feeling defeated before I even started.

"Some people feel safer regretting and not trying and they're okay going on with the status quo. So if that's you, then there's nothing you need to change. But," he leaned in and held my eyes, "I suspect that's not you. Is it?"

I blinked at him.

That was the very moment something inside me started to tip. I could feel it building in me. I was just sitting there on his couch, doing not a single thing to accomplish my dream other than feeling myself accelerate toward a decision. A decision I knew could take me on a completely different path than the one I was currently on.

I looked toward the windows. The sky was no longer black. It was a dark blue, that precursor to dawn.

It settled in me then, the genuine belief that I <u>could</u> do this, if I really wanted to.

From that moment to the moment I actually <u>did</u> choose, was maybe five seconds.

Isn't it funny how just five seconds can change our lives completely?

Kind of the way one night can.

Sitting there on his couch, my insides were barreling ahead toward something new and for the first time I wasn't trying to stop it at all.

I wanted it. Why couldn't I go for it? What did I have to lose, really? It wasn't like I was going to end up homeless or something. The only thing I had to lose was my pride, and I've lost that before, over things that were far less important.

My eyes sharpened on his. "I'd need a domain."

He grinned.

"If it's available," I added, slowly grinning myself.

"I have my laptop."

I smiled broadly and we hopped up together. I kept the blanket around my shoulders and followed his cute little naked ass across the living room and down the hall to his den. He sat at his desk and took me in his arms as I sat on his lap, cocooned in the blanket.

Once he got his laptop started up, we did some domain searching. My first several ideas were taken already. We spent half an hour brainstorming different ideas until we finally found a domain that was available and I bought it right on the spot, complete with WordPress hosting.

When I clicked "Buy" and watched the confirmation come through, I sat there on his lap, grinning at the screen. I was really going to do this.

I turned and looked at him and we smiled at each other. God, such a handsome, amazing man, this Grayson Piers.

"No turning back now." He winked at me.

I took his face in both my hands and planted an enthusiastic kiss on his lips.

"Mmm," he said when I pulled away, his eyebrows raised and his arms wrapping more firmly around that. "I like that. I wonder what you'll do to me after you pick out a blog template."

"Let's don't wait to find out." I kissed him again, feeling him growing against me. I was ready too. <u>Again</u>.

We'd cleaned him out of condoms, but since I was on birth control, we'd had a session 'in the raw.' I was ready for more.

Our kiss deepened and his strong arms supported me as I rearranged so I was straddling him. The blanket was in the way, but as he kissed me, he pulled the blanket up until I was exposed. I was open and ready for him, and felt his firm cock nearby, but he didn't enter me yet. Still under the blanket, his hands massaged my back and hips, working down and massaging my ass. Our tongues eagerly tasted each other. I ran my hands down his firm chest and to his hard nipples. I pinched them gently between my fingers and felt his cock bob against me in response.

His mouth broke away from mine and he moved to my neck. He sucked gently just below my earlobe. Working his way down my neck, he took my skin into his wet mouth and lit me up all over. I pressed my bare chest against his, arching my head back as he came to the crook of my neck. He sucked harder then, and I let out a shaky breath. My hands gripped his broad shoulders.

The lips of my sex were spread open and pulsing. I kept adjusting my hips slightly, seeking him, longing for touch. The tip of his cock was pressed against my inner thigh, just next to me, but he was purposely not coming inside me yet, teasing me.

I liked it. It made me want him even more.

He bent down toward my breasts and I leaned back to give him access. He cupped one breast with one hand, bringing it up to his mouth and sucking eagerly. I started to go limp with delight and would have sunk back. His hand on my back supported me and kept me close.

He got my other breast aching, then finally swung over to it. I moved it toward him so he'd get to it sooner. He took my hard nipple into his mouth and sucked on it, running his tongue around it in circles. By this time his cock was bobbing against me, against my outer lips, against my clit, against my opening, and away again. Every time I'd angle toward him, he'd pull just slightly away.

"Come on," I whispered, almost commanded.

"Come on what?" he asked quietly. I looked down to see him still attached to my breast, but his lips were curled into a mischievous grin.

"Brat."

He put both hands on my back, pulled me hard to his mouth and sucked firmly. I exhaled sharply.

"What do you want?" he murmured as he moved to my other breast. His hands moved down to my ass, spreading me open slightly. His cock lighted on my clit then was gone.

"You."

"Hmm?" he teased. "What?"

I firmly took his face between my hands, gave him a hard kiss, and said, "Get that cock inside me right now."

"Yes, ma'am," he said grinning. He reached between us, took hold of his cock, and aimed. He was dead center. Pressing my hips down with his free hand, he slid straight into my wet channel. I was so tight I felt every ridge of his rock-hard shaft as he entered me. I sighed with relief at having him fill me at last and he groaned, dropping his forehead onto my shoulder.

Taking my hips in both hands, he gripped me firmly, helping me ride him. He felt so good I didn't ever want it to stop. I wanted to feel him inside me and feel his arms around me and taste the skin on his neck and shoulders for the rest of time.

He grabbed the blanket, sliding it off my body and letting it fall to the floor. I was too hot to need it anymore. He sucked on my neck and thrust deep inside me. I don't know how I still had it within me, but I was so wet I'd soaked him and could hear the sounds of him driving into me.

"Make it last," I whispered, sucking his jaw then coming up to his mouth.

He kissed me fiercely as we opened wide to each other. He rubbed against me faster, bringing me higher. I moaned and worked against him, my whole body tingling. I was so close to the edge I thought I was about to go over.

He pulled out of me suddenly and I gasped.

He gave me a quick, impassioned kiss then looked at me with those smoldering blue eyes. "Get on the floor."

I lifted myself off his lap and got to my feet. He backed his chair away slightly and we moved to the open floor behind us. As we got down to our knees, he took me by the shoulders and turned me gently, so I was on all fours, facing away from him. I arched my pelvis up, opening to him.

He came behind me and placed one hand flat on the small of my back as he guided his cock into me. Pleasure washed over me and my arms bent slightly, my head falling down. He rocked me deeply and slowly at first, then escalated faster and faster. I arched back against him, wanting even more pressure. He grabbed my shoulders and hammered into me hard.

"Yes!" I gasped.

He wasn't even touching my throbbing clit but the pleasure was so hard and intense inside me I felt nearly ready to go over. He rammed into me again and again, gripping my shoulder with one hand and squeezing my breast with the other.

He gave me a few more thrusts, damn near sending me into heaven, then he released me and pulled out. I slowly collapsed onto my side, curling inward. I pressed my legs together to put mild pressure on my throbbing sex.

Panting, I rolled onto my back and looked at him. He was on his knees but sank back onto his heels. He was breathing heavily, his eyes smoldering and devouring me. His cock was bulging, nearly flat against his stomach, ready for me. I spread my legs, inviting him.

He came down on his hands, his muscles flexing as he got into position above me.

Our eyes locked for a moment. I couldn't believe how I wanted this man more and more. Not just his cock and his fucking sexy body, but him. I reached up and took his face in my hands, kissing him passionately. He sank onto me, his hand curling up into my hair as he kissed me back. Our bodies damp with sweat, he entered me again. I moaned in his mouth, still kissing him, grabbing the back of his hair. He rocked me firmly, and I didn't want him to stop.

Our mouths broke apart and we held each other's gaze as he continued to slide his hard cock in and out of me. I was building again, my chest flushing hot. As the pleasure ballooned in my body, my eyes closed helplessly.

"Look at me," he whispered.

I opened my eyes and saw him watching me, eagerly, tenderly.

He thrust into me again and the pleasure in my core spiked higher. Overcome, I closed my eyes again.

"Look at me," he whispered again.

His cock was straining harder against me and I gripped him firmly. The pleasure in my body climbed sharply. I opened my eyes and locked onto his. He was close, panting hard, his face reflecting the rising power between us.

He thrust into me harder and I opened my mouth in raw desire but kept my eyes on his. Straining hard against one another, his shaft took me and filled me completely. He came into me so deeply, each thrust landed with a burst of pleasure on my clit. We held each other's eyes and I watched his face as he climbed toward release. I let him watch me too, filled as I was with ecstasy.

I unbent my knees, open to him completely, arching myself toward him as he thrust into me again and again. Each thrust promised impending release and yet I rose higher. He grew harder. His face reflected unguarded desire and pleasure. My whole body felt hot and ready to burst and I thought I was literally going mad with pleasure and still he drove into me. I cried out once, twice, straining every time his hard cock slammed into me.

His movements grew suddenly frantic and he said, "Oh Chloe," and his eyes pinched shut. Just as his hot semen filled me I exploded into a climax that had me thrashing and crying out. He cried out too and released his full weight on me, grinding into me. My legs trembled as my orgasm tore through me, spiking hard against his cock. I clawed at his back helplessly, coming completely undone.

It seemed to go on forever, the pleasure bursting through me again and again. At last

I came down in slow, powerful waves that left my heart pounding fiercely and me gasping for breath. When it was over and we were weakly holding each other, panting into each other's necks, I was the first to speak.

"Holy god," I whispered.

He sank further against my neck then, wrapping me up firmly in his arms, and squeezed me like he couldn't get enough.

The phrase, "I love you," came suddenly to mind and I realized it would have felt as natural to say it as it would've been to hear it.

He came up slightly so he could look me in the eyes.

His eyes seemed to say what I was thinking. Perhaps mine did too.

He kissed me then, deeply and intimately. I kissed him in return, holding back nothing.

When he pulled away, he stayed close. He rolled onto his side, bringing me with him. I settled against his chest, still panting slightly. The sky out the window was getting lighter. The sun would be breaking the horizon soon.

It had felt so peaceful and promising. In that moment.

If only we could've stayed in that moment longer... long enough for my heart to be ready for him.

A breeze sweeps through the patio of the restaurant, rustling the palm trees and bringing the scent of the ocean. We've polished off the bruschetta and the calamari, but we're still nursing our drinks. "Okay, so go over the itinerary with us," Ashley says to Isabella. "I'm confused about tomorrow."

"Well tomorrow a lot of people are still arriving, so we thought it'd be fun to have one day where people could choose their activity. There's so much to do here. So there's a charter van going down to the beach and we'll provide surfboards and boogie boards and stuff for whoever wants to do that. There's wind surfing there too. Or people can just hang on the beach."

Sam raises her hand, "That's so what I would've done."

"Or there's the zip lining thing," Isabella says.

"I'm so excited about that!" I say.

Sam gapes at me. "You're going on it?"

I nod eagerly.

"On purpose?"

"It'll be fun. I've never done anything like that before."

"Look at you getting all bold," Ashley says with a grin. "First it's taking off to Boise, then it's the blogging thing, now it's zip lining. What will we see next from you?"

I smile at her. I have felt bolder lately. Since moving to Boise, I've taken myself out to dinner (a lot) and gone to movies all by myself and I don't feel weird about it at all. It's actually pretty fun. I'm not anti-social or anything; I've made a few work friends and we've gotten together a few times, too. But I've never been one to do something completely by myself. Not like I have been recently. It's a nice feeling, like I've finally grown into my own skin.

It's something I wish I could thank Grayson for. It's sometimes strange to me that in my quest to make sure I don't need a man, it was a man who gave me that shot of courage I needed. But he did.

I've wondered what my life would've been like if I'd been with a man like Grayson from the beginning instead of a man like Brad. But then again, maybe Brad was what I needed at the time. I'd spent so many years being the responsible one, Brad's inclination to be practical used to be an attraction. He was more responsible than a lot of kids my age. But those responsibilities I'd felt in life were placed on my shoulders too young, and they'd changed me. In some ways for the better. In some ways not. I've only recently rediscovered the more impulsive side of me. I'd forgotten about her.

In some ways, I have Grayson to thank for helping me get to know her again.

I still remember the way his eyes held mine as he encouraged me to lay plans. To be bold. Fearless.

The Night of Grayson wasn't really about any one moment. It was the sum total of every moment. It wasn't just the hottest sex I'd ever had. It was the fact that I'd never felt so physically open to a man before. It wasn't just that we talked more intimately and deeply than anyone should with a stranger, it was the fact that he didn't feel like a stranger. He felt like mine and I felt like his.

It was magical. It really was.

Which made what happened next all the more devastating.

Chapter 7

The Morning After the Night of Grayson

We'd been lying on the floor of his office on a little nest of blankets. Neither one of us had on a stitch of clothing, which had more or less been the case since we'd first taken them off. Nearly an hour had passed since the last time we had sex. Even though I was raw from so many encounters in such a short span of time, I knew I could get going again if I really wanted to.

He lay propped up on one elbow, his face close to mine, our legs entwined together. We were doing that lovers' dance I'd read about but never experienced.

We didn't say a word as our fingertips ran over cheekbones, shoulders, arms, chests. It wasn't sexual. It was tender, and we were doing more than exploring each other's bodies. I think I'd already sampled every bit of him by then anyway. We were knowing each other. Claiming each other.

At one point our eyes locked and our movements stopped. Our gaze went so deep, I almost felt we were entering each other somehow. Then he took my face in both of his hands and kissed me so tenderly it was like falling. He parted his lips and I responded by opening mine. His tongue touched mine and he rolled on top of me, embracing me in his arms. I both felt as if we were falling together and as if he'd caught me. If there'd been any part of me that had been resisting Grayson, it was gone in that moment.

I wrapped my arms around his neck and he stroked my side as we kissed deeply. His hardness grew against my thigh. The heat between my legs was instant, and only gave flight to everything else. In his arms, with his firm weight on top of me, my entire body was soaring. I opened to him and he entered me with one stroke. Like one long exhale.

We held each other tightly and made love, kissing and caressing and nuzzling each other as he rocked me. As our intensity grew, my feelings for him grew too. My chest feel like it was going to burst. I rose myself to meet him and opened more and more to him and felt every inch of him inside me. I honestly couldn't tell where my body ended and his began. We seemed to merge together and become one unit. The sensation startled and amazed me.

His thrusts grew more urgent and he held me more fiercely. He whispered my name in my ear. "Chloe."

He said it like a term of endearment.

"Grayson," I whispered.

"Chloe." His hot breaths warmed my neck and we moved together faster. "I want this forever," he said, and I burned for him both body and soul. "I want you."

I want you too.

I clung to him and he held me in his strong arms, stroking me until I caught fire. He said my name once more as we exploded into a joint orgasm. His hard cock pulsed against me as the pleasure overtook me. It stretched out in wave after wave. I was completely consumed. White pinpricks of light danced on the edge of my vision. At last the waves began to retreat and I clutched him as the power of my orgasm began to relent. He was still stroking me, softly and slowly, drawing the remaining bits of pleasure out of my body.

By the time I lay loosely in his arms, completely spent, my world had changed forever.

We were both panting, coming down from the high. I looked into those blue eyes and he smiled. His lone dimple appeared on his cheek. I reached up and touched it gently with the tip of my finger. I was still lightheaded and weak.

We held each other's eyes. With only the sound of our ragged breathing in the background, I looked at Grayson as he looked at me. I thought he was going to tell me he loved me.

My heart began to pound. To this day, I couldn't tell you if it was due to longing or fear.

Finally he took a breath, ready to speak. If he told me he loved me, I honestly didn't know what I would say back.

But this is what he said: "I used to think my parents were crazy."

My eyebrows shot up in surprise, then I laughed. "Well, that's not what I expected you to say."

"What did you expect me to say?"

His question caught me off guard and I looked at him frankly, wondering if he could see it on my face. There was a pregnant pause. He kept his eyes on mine, but stroked my hair gently.

"I don't know." I smiled, keeping it playful. "I guess I didn't expect your parents to come into the conversation so soon after we... you know."

"You know?" he asked, his eyes twinkling at my hesitation to come right out with it.

"Okay, okay. Tonight you've given me the fucking of a lifetime."

He smiled broadly and puffed up his chest, looking perfectly pleased with himself. "Fucking of a lifetime, huh?" He twirled a lock of my auburn hair around his fingers. "Don't build me up too much or I'll be doomed to spend the rest of our lives trying to top an impossible standard."

My heart started pounding against my chest so loud I knew he had to hear it. The rest of our lives?

"So why did you think your parents were crazy?" I asked with a smile, trying to deflect this huge thing I felt building between us.

"Did I tell you my parents were eighteen when they got married?"

My ear caught on the word 'married.' I shook my head. "You said they've been together twenty years or something."

"Thirty. And they've been miserable for most of it, as far as I can tell."

I furrowed my brow. He wasn't kidding.

"Miserable." He nodded. "And I swore I would never end up like that. Who gets married when they're eighteen? How can anyone think they're not going to screw up a decision like that when they're not even done growing up yet? It's stupid. Almost as stupid as sticking it out for thirty years and hating the one person in the world you're really, really supposed to love."

"I'm sorry. That must've been hard." One of the things that comforted me after my mother's death was knowing how much my

96

parents had loved each other. While somewhat recovered and relatively happy, six years after my mother's death, my father still won't date.

"Eh. I'm pretty adaptable," Grayson said. "You learn to get along on your own when you're the last kid in a long line of kids. My parents were worn out and kinda checked out by the time I hit junior high. I made a lot of decisions for myself, and one of them was that I'd never get married young. I promised myself I wouldn't marry before thirty."

"Thirty??"

"My friends call it The Rule. They like to kinda mess with me about it. But did you know the human brain isn't even done developing until you're twenty-five? I figured thirty's a safe cushion."

I shook my head again. "I'm twenty-three. I've got two years to go until I'm done developing." I gave him a devilish grin.

His eyes slid down to my chest. "I think you've developed just fine, sweetheart."

"You're almost twenty-five. Less than a year to go."

"Six until I'm thirty." I guess that sounds like he could've been giving me the brush off, like, <u>Don't even think about it honey, I'm nowhere near thirty.</u>

But he wasn't. And I knew it.

He looked deep into my eyes, placed his hand on my cheek, and leaned in until he was nearly kissing me. "I may have to make an exception."

He kissed me then, with my heart beating out of my chest. I don't know where the hell my brain went, because it was definitely my heart in control at that moment. I kissed him back so deeply it was like my heart was saying <u>yes</u> to a question he hadn't even asked.

When he pulled back he leaned on his elbow again looking content and satisfied. "Are you hungry?"

I nodded, too stunned by the moment to speak. My heart was still pounding. What was I getting into?

"How about I take a quick shower, then I'll make you my famous French toast."

"And bacon?" I smiled back at him as if my head weren't spinning.

"Anything you want." He gave me another peck before hopping to his feet.

I rolled onto my stomach, watching his bare feet pad across the carpet to the doorway.

He stopped and looked down at me with that crooked smile of his. "Feel free to join me in the shower," he said, "if you have the strength." He winked and left the room.

In the five seconds that followed his departure from my presence, a cold wave of fear dropped over me.

Right there on Grayson's floor.

Funny isn't it? Just how much can happen in five seconds?

I suddenly realized that only three months earlier I was prepared to marry another man and here I was, ready to give my heart to Grayson after one day. I really was. And I did not doubt he intended to give his heart to me. I thought of him whispering in my ear: <u>I want this forever. I want you.</u>

I thought of his Rule and him saying, <u>I may have to make an exception.</u>

Shaking, I got to my feet and tiptoed to the hall. Down the way, through an open bedroom door, I heard the shower water running.

In the opposite direction was the living room and my clothes. And the door.

I wrapped my arms around myself, shivering. Not from the cold. I don't know how long I stood there, deciding.

I had said I didn't want a one-night stand because I knew I had to be me, just me. Just for a while. I couldn't lose myself in a man again.

But...

I looked in the direction of his room.

But it's Grayson.

It was very clear to me, in that moment, that if I stayed, I would be wrapped up in Grayson for good. There would be no taking things slow. We were far past that point already. I knew I wouldn't be able to resist him.

I took a slow, indecisive step backwards, toward the living room. And another. Spurred on by the momentum of those two steps, I backed farther and farther away, making myself do it, until I was bolting into

Grayson's kitchen and fumbling to get dressed.

I ran out of his house, fully dressed but with my shoes in my hands. I drove barefoot, away from Grayson's house and down through the hills, my heart pounding.

It took every ounce of strength I had not to turn around and go back. As I crossed Swan Pointe, heading for my apartment, I had to make the decision over again every time I went through an intersection. I pulled into my apartment complex knowing he was probably out of the shower by now. And I wasn't there. I was here.

I would not permit myself to cry. I had to be strong. I couldn't be one of those women who couldn't survive without a man. I wouldn't.

When I pulled into my parking spot, I was momentarily distracted by the fact that Ashley's car was still parked out front. Shouldn't she have taken Isabella to the airport by now? And after that, Ashley was supposed to drive back to her apartment in Rosebrook. What happened?

"Where the hell have you been?" Ashley demanded when I opened the door to find her sitting on my couch.

The room was empty. I dropped my bag and shoes on the floor, furrowing my brows at her. "Why aren't you on the road? Where's Isabella?"

"I dropped her off at the airport but then came back here to wait for you. Why didn't you answer my texts? Is your phone dead?"

Then Ashley took in my clothes—and probably my just-been-fucked appearance—and a dawning smile broke out across her face.

"Ah!" she said in a Sam-like way. "I see!"

"Ashley—"

Her phone rang and she pulled it out of her back pocket, still looking gleeful. Suddenly worn out, I headed toward my bedroom when I heard "Bella? She's here. Spent the night with some lucky guy from the looks of it."

I spun on Ashley and heard Isabella squealing through the phone. "Shut up, Ashley!" but Isabella's squealing reached a new decibel level as Ashley put it on speaker phone.

"Oh my god!" Isabella said. "I want details."

"Absolutely not."

Ashley's face immediately registered concern. "Are you okay? What'd he do to you?"

I turned around and tried, once more, for my bedroom. "Nothing."

"Nothing?"

I heard Ashley get off the couch and start following me. I managed not to groan in frustration.

"Well, I mean, yeah we did something but he didn't do anything wrong." God, I did not want to talk about it.

"What's going on?" I heard Isabella ask through the phone.

"Chloe's upset," Ashley said.

"I'm not upset."

I'm not sure why I couldn't tell them. I tell them everything. Ashley was the first one I ran to when Brad called things off. My Firework Girls came and cried with me and got me to laugh and feel like things would be okay, in the end.

But in that moment, I couldn't begin to put into words what happened and what I was feeling and I didn't want to try. I just wanted to go to bed and sleep. For a month.

"It was a night of sex and it was great but now it's over and I want to go to bed. I haven't slept a wink."

I got to my door and glanced back over my shoulder to see if Ashley was ready to let things lie. She was grinning again. "Wait until Sam hears about this."

"Don't," I said strongly, before I could stop myself.

I turned and Ashley was still grinning, but giving me a puzzled expression. "Why not?"

"Look, I—" I sighed. God, I was just so tired. "Thank you for getting me through my Not Wedding night. You too, Bella. But can we please, please not talk about it again? I just want to move on, okay?"

"Okay," Isabella said. "I understand."

Ashley nodded but I avoided her eyes. It felt like she was still scrutinizing me.

"Okay," she said. "Well, since I know you're okay, I'm going to head back."

"Sorry for not answering my phone."

"It's okay," she said giving me a hug. "I'll text you when I get there."

I pulled it together enough to smile before she left. I said goodbye to both her and Isabella and then she was gone and that was it.

I was standing alone in the middle of my apartment with the smell of Grayson on my skin and the memory of him all around me.

I wondered what he was doing in that moment. I wondered how he reacted when he came out of the shower to find me gone. This is something I've wondered many, many times in the months since.

I pulled my phone from my pocket and checked for a text from him before remembering he didn't have my number and I didn't have his. Of course there were no messages from him, only Ashley's increasingly frantic texts that morning and a few from Isabella begging me to text Ashley before she called the police.

I dropped my phone on the couch and didn't bother plugging it in to charge even though the battery was almost dead. I walked back to my bedroom. I wondered if Grayson was eating French toast anyway. Without me.

Just like he'd go on with the rest of his life. Without me.

It's for the best, I thought, and collapsed on my bed fully dressed. I didn't allow myself to cry.

In fact, I have never once allowed myself to cry for Grayson Piers.

As I've said, I had to be strong.

Chapter 8

The waiter has cleared away our platters, but we're in no hurry to leave. The girls and I are chatting happily when I get a text from my brother.

Bobby: Almost there.

Me: Okay. We're in the Sandbar finishing up appetizers and cocktails. You're welcome to join us if you like.

I don't get an answer back and take to checking the open patio doors that lead toward the lobby.

A minute later someone I know does walk through the doors. But it isn't Bobby.

Walking smoothly onto the patio, his eyes sweep the area like he's looking for someone. His eyes land for a moment on Sam. There's a brief flicker of recognition, but then he sees me and instantly stops short.

Grayson.

I don't think my heart is beating anymore. I know I'm not breathing. I'm confronted with such a confusing array of emotions I feel physically slapped.

I can't move at all. He looks as shocked as I feel. There's a sudden sharpness in his eyes. Anger. And it's directed right at me. <u>Oh god.</u>

There's this moment when I'm torn between wanting to run away in horror after what I did to him, and wanting to launch myself into his arms and beg him to forgive me.

This is what happens in the next moment.

Sam glances toward the door and says, "Oh, there he is!"

It happens in slow motion and is as confusing and disorienting as a dream. Sam hops out of her chair. His eyes go to her and his expression changes. He looks like he's still trying to recover from his shock, but he does a fair job of it. Better than me. I'm watching it all unfold with my mouth hanging open. He's smiling. At Sam. I don't understand why until she goes up to him and puts her arms around him and kisses him right on the lips.

That's when my heart stops again and I look away. I can't breathe. My heart hurts. It really hurts and I don't think it's beating.

Oh god, can a person die from shock?

She leads him back to our table and I hitch my mouth into a smile, trying to look normal. Do I look normal?

"Girls, this is Grayson. Grayson these are my girlfriends, Ashley, Chloe—" his eyes flit to mine and I try to look normal, am I still smiling?—"and the lovely bride, Isabella."

Then I remember. He's met them before. Everyone but Sam. He and Mr. Greek God came right up to our table there in the Perched Owl.

The girls apparently don't remember because they say some variation of the whole "nice to meet you" routine.

"Where's your stuff?" Sam asks him.

His eyes flick away from mine and he looks at her. My Grayson is looking at My Sam and her arm is still around his waist. I can't feel my body.

"I left my suitcase in the car. I figured I'd find out where our room is first."

Our room??

Oh my holy fucking god, if you have any mercy, strike me down right now.

"I'll take you," she says, leading him away. She glances back over her shoulders and gives us a wink.

I watch them go. He doesn't turn back. They just disappear, on their way to get his suitcase and take it to their room where Sam's going to do god knows what to him.

I take a sip of my water with trembling hands. I really can't breathe.

"He's cute," Isabella says.

"He looks kind of familiar," Ashley says.

I look at her in alarm.

She catches my expression and gives me a look of concern.

Oh, did I forget to keep the fake smile plastered on my face?

I pull my lips into a smile but it feels funny. Am I smiling?

"You okay?"

I stand and give a fake laugh. I even bat my hand at her like an idiot and say, "Of

110

course, of course. Yes, I'm fine I just have to... go to my room for... something."

I'm walking away from the table on unsteady legs.

"Uh... okay," Ashley says. "See you at dinner."

I raise one arm in acknowledgement but keep walking.

I exit the patio and make it to the sprawling lobby. It's when I'm stuck waiting for the elevator that I realize I might see him.

Them.

I glance around but they're nowhere in sight. At his car maybe? Has she been to his house? Has she been all over his house the way I was?

I feel physically ill.

I punch the button again. I don't want them to come in and see me standing here but I don't know where else to go. I just have to get to my room.

The elevator dings and I squeeze through as soon as the gap is big enough to admit me. I'm punching the round "7" button before the doors even finish opening.

I punch it again. Then the "Close door" button. Why do those never, ever work? What's even the point of them? I glance at the lobby again, which I have a clear view of because the doors are still all the way open. I still don't see them. As I'm pummeling the "7" button, the doors finally close and I'm on my way.

As I clear the lobby level, the glass back of the compartment opens up to provide a view of the grounds and, as the car goes higher, the coast. I was enjoying this view earlier, when I'd checked in and brought my suitcase up to the room, but I keep my back to it now. I'm gripping the brass hand rail and bending part way over.

I can hardly think. All I can see in my mind is Grayson and Sam kissing each other hello then walking off together. My Grayson and my Sam.

The car dumps me out on the seventh floor and I rush down the hallway to my room. I fumble with the key card—red light, red light, green—and swing the door open. When I shut it behind me, I collapse against it and slide all the way to the floor.

Grayson is here. He's here at Isabella's wedding with Sam and I think I'm going to just have to stay in my room forever or else catch a plane to Bermuda or something. What in the hell just happened?

I sit there stunned, my heart pounding soundly in my ears, when there's a sharp rap at the door.

I jump and let out an audible gasp.

I freeze, my heart falling down on the job again as it stops beating.

What if it's Grayson? What if it's Sam?

I sit there frozen another few seconds. There's another knock, this time followed by Ashley's voice, "Chloe? You okay?"

I scramble to my feet and open the door enough to peek out and verify it's really her and that she's alone.

"What's going on?" she asks.

I open the door all the way and gesture her in. She comes in, giving me a questioning look, and I close the door behind her. Still hanging on to the door knob, I close my eyes and take a deep breath, trying to steel myself.

"Chloe—" she begins.

"It's him." I grasp my hands together and hold them to my chest. "He's the guy."

"Who? What guy?"

"Grayson." I don't know that I've ever said his name aloud. Not since I was with him. "Sam's guy."

"Yeah, who is that guy?" Ashley asks. "He looks so familiar. Did he go to Hartman with us?"

I shake my head impatiently. "We met him and another guy at the Perched Owl, remember? On the night of my—"

"—Not Wedding!" Her eyes light up as the mystery is solved. "That's right!" Her expression falls again, trying to figure out what that has to do with my distraught state.

"He's the guy."

A dawning look falls over Ashley's face, followed by a look of horror. "Oh my god."

I put my hands over my face. "What am I going to do?"

"He's the guy?"

I nod, my hands still over my face.

"The guy you slept with?"

I groan. "What am I going to do?"

"Okay," Ashley says firmly. I slowly lower my hands to look at her. "Okay," she says again, "let's just... think for a minute."

She leads me over to the bed and we sit down.

We both take a deep breath.

"So..." Ashley begins, then stops.

I nod. What in the hell can either one of us say?

"Um..." she says, then nothing.

"Ashley," I say desperately, "What do I do? Do I tell her?"

"Ugh. I don't know. Let's... just... back up a second." She takes another deep breath. "Are you... interested in him or anything?"

Interested? What difference does it make? I <u>ran out</u> on him, and I did not miss the anger in his eyes when he saw me. Who can blame him? To top it off, he's clearly gotten over it since he's here as Sam's fucking <u>date.</u> "Things ended really badly between us. Plus, it was, you know, just one night."

"Okay, then it's not like you want to be with him or something." I swallow hard. "So, this situation obviously isn't... <u>ideal</u>. But, like you said, it was just a one-night stand so it's not like he's your ex or something."

I blink at her and nod stupidly. That's what it would be for a normal person anyway, right? Just a one-night stand and nothing more. In my weakened state, I'm not terribly inclined to admit I'm the kind of girl who falls for a guy after <u>one night.</u>

"And..." she seems to be casting around, trying to catch her thoughts, "Sam didn't know so she didn't do anything wrong."

"God no. This isn't Sam's fault."

It's mine, mine, mine.

"And..." Ashley continues, "it's not like we need to worry about her getting all serious about him because she doesn't get serious about anybody. He'll probably be in and out of here as fast as all of her other guys. So..."

Ashley let's her sentence trail off and takes a deep breath.

"As far as the whole..." she gives me an uncomfortable look, "...<u>sharing</u> the same guy thing, knowing Sam, the damage has probably already been done."

I groan and cover my face with my hands again. Oh god, the thought of them together literally hurts. And let me tell you, I've been down this road before when that bastard Brad cheated on me. But the thought of Grayson with Sam... I pinch my eyes against the mental image that springs unwanted to my mind.

"What do I do?" I groan. "I have no idea what to do."

It's quiet for a moment, then Ashley says gently, "I think this comes down to you and whether you can... handle this or not."

I look at her and she shrugs sympathetically.

"If you can deal with it, you could just not say anything and it'll all be over soon. She'll probably be sick of him by week's end anyway. I was kinda shocked she even agreed to the full five days."

I nod. It's a whole lot of one guy for Sam's taste.

"But if you can't handle it, just tell her. She'll send him packing."

I sigh. Sam would, if I said something. But I don't know if I can tell her. Do I really want that kind of thing going down during Isabella's wedding? And is it fair to rob Sam of her plans when, let's face it, I blew it with Grayson a long time ago? It's not like I'm trying to claim territorial rights. He's not mine to claim and never was. Right? What right have I to be selfish about it when, like Ashley said, the damage has already been done. It feels selfish to ruin Sam's week (not to mention Isabella's) just because of my drama.

But, a little dark corner of myself admits, I selfishly <u>don't</u> want to tell her, because if I tell her she'll send him away and I don't want him to go. As fucked up as that is, this tiny, horrible part of me can't bear the thought of him leaving.

But can I bear the thought of him staying, and all that implies?

I sigh. "What would you do?"

Ashley absently runs her hand down her long braid, bringing it in front of her shoulder and playing with the end. "I don't know. This is a tough one. But... you know, it's too late to avoid the ick factor. I think since he's really not that important to either one of you, I'd maybe just let it slide. But Chloe, it really does come down to what you think you can handle. You're the one who's going to have to deal with it."

I sit there for a while, debating with myself. The one thing I'd like to do—go back in time and make this not happen—isn't really an option. So either I tell Sam (not appealing) or I suck it up and just try to get through the weekend (also not appealing).

The longer I sit there, the more I come down from the initial shock and the more I think I might need to just keep my mouth shut. Sam didn't do anything wrong. Why should she have to suffer?

And Grayson is clearly no longer an option for me either, no matter how much I may regret that fact. While I haven't dated or been interested in dating anyone because I haven't been able to get him out of my system yet, he's obviously moved on. Do I really want to yank the rug out from underneath him once again? How callous would that be?

I glance out my window. The grassy grounds are covered with flowers and Bird of Paradise bushes and softly swaying palms. The sea beyond is glittering yellow in the late afternoon sun.

"It's Isabella's wedding," I say finally. "I'm not going to risk ruining it. And we're here in this amazing place that I've really been looking forward to enjoying." I give Ashley a weak smile. "I'll let them have their fun and I'll try to have mine."

"Good for you." She pats my knee.

"But... tomorrow." I don't think I can handle dinner with everyone. I'm just going to order room service, binge watch some cooking shows, and get myself geared up for the rest of the week. "I'll text them and let them know I'm not feeling well so you don't have to make excuses for me. Tomorrow, I'll be ready to go."

Ashley watches me carefully. "You sure?"

I nod, then smile. "It'll be okay. It'll be a fun week, right?"

I don't believe that yet, but I'm determined to believe it by tomorrow.

After Ashley leaves, I send out a few texts and order room service. By the time I'm curled up on the bed watching TV and eating

120

a most delicious chicken and mushroom quesadilla, I damn near have myself convinced it really is going to be okay.

I'm a stronger woman now. I can do this.

Right?

Chapter 9

The next morning as I'm getting ready, a rather terrifying thought occurs to me. I immediately dive for my phone and text Ashley.

Me: What if he told Sam?

My heart pounds as I watch my phone, waiting for her reply. What if he told Sam? What if she's mad at me for not telling her first? My phone dings.

Ashley: Has Sam said anything to you?

Me: No.

Ashley: Then she doesn't know.

That's true. If Sam knew, I'd know it. God, I hate this.

Ashley: If he was going to say something, I think he'd done it by now.

Me: Yeah. Okay.

I'm relieved, but not. I don't know that I like keeping this from Sam.

I go through all my reasoning from last night to see if it still holds. Should I just go ahead and tell her? But in the end I come to the same conclusion. Saying something would only mean drama for Sam, Grayson, and possibly Isabella, and for what? To spare my feelings over a guy I can't even have? I need to just suck it up and eventually Grayson will be out of everyone's life and it'll be over.

My heart clenches at the thought of Grayson being out of my life again, but then I snap myself out of it. It's not like he's <u>in</u> my life now. He's here with Sam. I just need to deal with it.

I consider skipping the zip line and going to the beach with Isabella and Ashley instead. I know Sam and Grayson are going on the zip line. I'm not sure I can handle being <u>that</u> close.

But after a few minutes' consideration, I decide against it. That's what the old Chloe would do: run. Go the safe route. Trying out the zip line is the thing I've been looking forward to most, aside from seeing Isabella marry the man of her dreams. I've been wanting to go, so I'm going.

I can do this.

The resort's massive and luxurious lobby is humming with people, including a crowd that's here for Isabella's wedding, from what I can tell. Among the many strangers, I see familiar faces: Isabella and Shane, her parents, a few other family members I met yesterday, my brother, my girls and, yes, there's Grayson too. The crowd seems to be roughly divided into two groups, though one is significantly smaller than the other.

I go to Isabella's group first, to apologize for missing dinner last night.

"Are you feeling better?" she asks and I nod. She looks stunning in white shorts and a blue midriff top. She's obviously wearing a string bikini underneath, since the tie behind her neck is visible. Shane has his arm around her waist. They're both positively glowing and I can't help but smile at it. I wonder

124

again if I should go with them. Seeing her so happy is lightening my mood, for sure.

But I really did want to try that zip line. If I don't go, I'm just going to feel like I'm chickening out.

I chat with them a minute, then excuse myself. I take a resolute breath and go up to the other, smaller group. I stop on the outskirts even though Sam and the others are still several feet away from me.

No need to get too close.

"Is this for the van to the zip line?" I ask the guy next to me. I think he's one of Isabella's many cousins, but I'm not sure. He looks maybe a couple years younger than my brother.

He says yes just as Sam catches my eye and waves me over. Grayson's standing right next to her but they're not touching, thank god.

I steel myself. I can do this.

I smile at her, thank the kid, and head over, trying not to look at Grayson even though I sense him watching me approach.

Bobby is there too, chatting with a girl with big blonde hair and a bright pink shorts outfit. She looks like a big bag of cotton candy. She even has on big hoop earrings and heels. Where in the hell does she think she's going in that outfit?

Bobby looks a little too absorbed in this girl for my taste. I say hi to Sam and Grayson—grateful for a reason to keep it brief—then put my hand on Bobby's arm, drawing his attention.

He sees me and smiles. "Hey, you made it. Feeling better?"

"Yeah." I accept a hug from him. Miss Cotton Candy gives me a cold, appraising look, taking in my denim shorts and olive green tank top.

<u>Oh please.</u> Who is this girl?

"Chloe, this is Scarlett," Bobby says. Scarlett? Seriously? This day just gets better and better. She's giving me that thinly-veiled, stay-away-from-my-territory look. "She's Shane's cousin," Bobby continues. "Scarlett, this is my sister, Chloe."

"Oh!" she says, in a ridiculously high voice, her face lighting up. "Your <u>sister!</u> Well, hi sweetie." She launches at me and envelopes me in a hug. I try not to cough, surrounded in a cloud of her perfume. "I'm sure we'll get to be fast friends!"

"Uh huh." I'm trying not to be impolite, but she's already gone back to being absorbed in my little brother. Idiot that he is, he's lapping it up. What is it with the male species sometimes?

"There are the vans," Grayson says.

My eyes swing to his face involuntarily. It's the first time I've looked at him—really looked at him, close up—since he got here. I can't keep my heart from reacting, but I'm trying to settle it down. I really am.

He's not looking at me, and wasn't talking to me specifically. Just the group. He nods his head toward the circular drive in front of the lobby, which we can see through the big glass windows. Indeed, there are a couple of large, luxurious-looking charter vans pulling in. They're actually more like little busses than vans.

"Okay everybody." Shane's commanding but friendly voice booms over the crowd. "The vans are here. The first one will take you down to the beach with us. The second goes up to the zip line. Have fun. We'll see you back here for dinner. Six o'clock."

Some people in the crowd start shuffling toward the lobby doors, while others are a little slower getting started.

"I actually think I'd rather go to the beach," Sam says.

Grayson and I both look at her.

"I'm not really a zip line fan." She seems a little irritated, but I'm not sure because she gives Grayson a smile.

"You're not coming?" Grayson asks, clearly surprised she's backing out.

"Don't worry, you won't be alone," she says lightly, but I can see the determination underneath. She puts her hand on his chest and smiles at him. I frown. "Bobby will keep you company. You two seemed to hit it off at dinner last night."

I glance at Bobby. He hasn't heard a word, absorbed as he is with Miss Cotton Candy. My frown deepens.

"And you can get to know Chloe." Sam gestures to me.

Grayson and I exchange glances. I can't figure out which I feel more right now: panic or irritation. I think I see a glimpse of something like panic in Grayson's eyes too.

"You said you'd come," Grayson says, returning to Sam.

Maybe he thinks he can persuade her to change her mind, but it's pretty clear to me there's no going back now. He can either go with Sam or go zip lining alone, but she's not coming. Apparently he hasn't yet figured out that Sam does what Sam wants to do and not one thing more.

But the joke's really on me, because here's what I just figured out.

By not telling Sam about my history with Grayson, I've basically given over "rights" to her. I mean, I know it shouldn't matter, because it's not like I have any sort of a future with him anyway. But keeping my mouth shut is the same thing as saying, "He's yours."

My head's spinning a bit because I've basically turned the tables on myself. If Sam gets tired of Grayson (which she's likely to do), and if I decided to at least <u>try</u> to mend things between us, <u>I'd </u>be the one breaking the friend rule. Not Sam.

"You have fun," Sam says lightly. "I'll see you when you get back." She goes up on her tiptoes to plant a kiss on him. And he kisses her back. Right in front of me.

Fuck. If that's not a clear message, I don't know what is. What the hell am I even worrying about? It's <u>over</u> with Grayson and has been since the moment I walked out on him.

I avert my eyes away from their kiss. My eyes land, unfortunately, on my baby brother tossing an arm around Miss Cotton Candy's shoulders and whispering something in her ear. I can't hear a word, but based on the looks on their faces and the ridiculous giggle now issuing forth from her mouth, I get the general idea.

Whatever.

I head for the door. I don't care who comes and who doesn't. I'm going and I don't need a freaking escort. Sam and Grayson can figure things out on their own. Why should I care?

I step through the rotating door and toward the charter van. It's a glorious California day and I am not going to let Sam or Grayson or anyone else get under my skin.

I hear Miss Cotton Candy and her giggling coming through the doors. I glance back and see her and my brother arm in arm. Grayson's nowhere in sight. Maybe he's going to the beach with Sam.

Good. Fine. Whatever.

I turn away and take a deep breath of fresh sea air. I'm just going to do my own thing. I know how to be single. I'm okay getting on the van by myself and having a grand time.

There are four guides near the van doors, handing people forms and pens. One guide—a surprisingly squat, heavy-set man—hands me one and I look it over. It's the consent form. I'd already read it online so I sign it straight away. Meanwhile, the guide is trying to explain why Miss Cotton Candy can't go zip lining in high heels and hoop earrings.

She's trying to argue, but one of the other guides steps in—a cute, athletic guy with an easy-going air of authority—and kindly tells her she can either change her shoes or stay behind.

I turn my back to the drama and climb the steps. I walk down the narrow aisle and slide across a soft leather seat to the window. I'm purposely not looking toward the lobby doors to see if Sam and Grayson have come out or what bus they might be heading toward. I'm looking determinedly out the window. The drive circles a small, well-kept pond with the resort's famous pair of white swans floating in the middle.

That's what I'm looking at when he climbs on board, alone. I sense him, and then see him out of the corner of my eye. The hair raises on my arm, like a little radar warning me of his presence.

As if I needed any help knowing.

He sits on the bench in front of me, but doesn't slide over to the window. I grip my hands in my lap and watch the swans gliding lazily on the water. The four guides climb on board and the cute authoritative one says we'll have a slight delay. Bobby and his fluffy pink girl haven't boarded the van yet, but ten minutes later they finally climb on board and the doors shut at last.

As they pass me in the aisle, taking the bench behind me, I notice she's missing her earrings and has changed into pink Keds. I get a whiff of her perfume.

The guides introduce themselves, give us a friendly welcome, and tell us to settle in and get ready for a fun day. This accomplished, they take their seats and the van pulls away from the hotel.

Only then do I look at Grayson's profile... wishing.

Chapter 10

The van heads northeast and climbs into the hills. Soon we're driving along a road lined with green trees on one side and occasional views of the sea on the other. Now that I've started glancing at Grayson's profile, I can't stop.

Maybe fifteen minutes into the drive, I brave speaking to him.

"Have you ever been zip lining before?"

His head moves slightly in my direction, but he doesn't turn around. In fact, he faces all the way forward again. At first I don't think he's going to answer. I'm about to return to my window when he says, "A few times."

His voice is tense, not surprisingly. It hurts anyway. I remember how his voice sounded when he said my name that night.

I press forward. I can't help myself. "Is it scary?" I'm careful to make my voice sound normal.

Again, I don't think he's going to answer me, but his face softens a bit. When he speaks, his voice isn't quite as hard. "Are you afraid of heights?"

"Not really."

"You'll be fine."

He could be talking to anyone, there's so little familiarity in his voice. Maybe it was a mistake to try to talk to him. Why did I?

"Though," he adds, "you don't strike me as the zip lining type."

I couldn't say for sure, but I get the feeling he said that just to get under my skin. It kinda sorta worked.

"Well, I'm full of surprises," I say firmly.

"Yeah, no kidding." I can only see his profile, but his face has hardened. I immediately regret my remark.

I glance behind me. Freaking Bobby is still wrapped up in Miss Cotton Candy and not paying attention to my conversation.

I lower my voice and lean toward Grayson slightly. "Grayson," I say softly, pleadingly. He glances at me out of the corner of his eyes, but doesn't turn his head. "I..."

"Hey, no big deal."

I frown and lean back against my seat. The minutes drag on in silence. I look back out the window. There's nothing but trees now, and no more views to the sea.

Grayson and I don't speak for the rest of the drive.

We finally get to the top and unload at the first platform. Here, we start putting on our harnesses, helmets, and gloves. It's nice to have something to do besides stare at the back of Grayson's head (or determinedly try <u>not</u> to stare, take your pick, because I was doing both).

The sturdy, wooden platform is near the top of a wooded incline. The line runs slightly downward to another platform some three hundred feet away. We're presented a gorgeous view of the mountain, valley, and the trees, but no view of the sea yet.

This first run is relatively short. From what I read online, the runs start out short and get longer, apparently to help newcomers get used to things first. There are eight runs altogether, working their way back down the mountain and to the coast.

The guides divide the crowd roughly into two, with two guides each. Grayson's eyes meet mine as we realize we've just been put into the same group. As there's still some shuffling going on, I consider switching groups to make things more comfortable for both of us. But he's not looking at me with hardness or anger or really any emotion I can define. He's just kind of... looking at me.

Acceptance. That's what it is.

I'm here and he's here and we're here together and we're going to be in the same group. Maybe we can handle that.

I stay where I am. One of our guides calls us up onto the platform and Grayson pulls his eyes away from mine at last.

I exhale quietly through my lips.

Okay. I can do this.

Then I get onto the platform, with the front edge leading to a sizeable drop, and I'm not so sure I can do this at all. Forget Grayson. How high up are we?

I cautiously shuffle nearer to the railing at the front and look over. Oh god, what was I thinking? That's a fucking <u>long</u> way down. I'm starting to wonder if Sam didn't have the right idea after all.

I examine the cable leading from our platform to the next one. Why is the cable so saggy? I thought it'd be more taut. Is that normal?

The guides don't seem too concerned. The cute one I saw laying down the law over a certain pair of high-heels earlier—Connor, I think he said his name was—asks if there are any first-timers in the group. My hand shoots up, along with Miss Cotton Candy (who suddenly seems much more friendly in my eyes), a middle-aged couple, and a guy who's maybe thirty.

The rest of the group—some five people including Grayson and my brother—are around my age and looking relaxed and excited. The only people I remember meeting are the middle-aged couple, who are related to Shane but I don't remember how, exactly.

"Okay," Cute Connor the Guide says, "no need to worry. We'll go over exactly how this is going to work."

I pay close attention as he gives us the instructions. He's both easy-going and confident, something that's setting me a little more at ease. He likes to say 'don't worry.' As in, "If you can't slow down at the end, don't worry, we'll catch you." And, "If you get stuck on the line, use your gloved hand to bring yourself in, like this. But don't worry if you can't pull yourself in, we'll come get you."

It's a little weird for him to be so calm and collected about things like not being able to slow down and getting stuck on a little wire way, way, <u>way</u> above those teeny, tiny trees down there.

I close my eyes and take a breath. Okay. I gotta stop psyching myself out. People do this all the time, right?

I look at the people who've done this before. I almost startle at the sight of

Grayson. I practically forgot he was here. Okay. It's alright. See how relaxed they all look? It'll be fine.

He gives me a slightly puzzled look.

What? I think. I'll be fine.

I return my attention to Cute Connor who gives us a dazzling smile and says, "That's it! I'll go first and demonstrate."

He and the other guide unhook a rope that's blocking the opening that leads to the rest of the platform. They re-hook the rope, to make sure none of the rest of us wander out nilly willy onto that little Launch Pad before it's time, I suppose.

Cute Connor steps up to the other guide, the squat one with a bit of a potbelly, and reassuringly strong-looking arms. I think his name is Frank. Or is it Felix? Forest?

"All you have to do is stand here," Connor says, "and Fred here will hook you up."

Fred. Yep, that's it. Fred attaches Connor's harness carabiner to the line, then he attaches the safety strap to the line.

That's right. Two straps. That's good. I'm okay with two straps.

140

Connor shows us how to hang on with our gloved hand to help keep our body straight and, later, to brake.

"Those of you who want to ride freestyle and try some tricks," he says grinning, "feel free."

Tricks? I think he must be kidding, but some guys who've gone before start high-fiving each other.

I'm starting to wish I'd done more than watch just the tutorial video on the website. I thought about going to YouTube and looking for more, but I was afraid I'd freak myself out, especially if I came across videos with titles like "Man Plunges to Death in Zip Line Accident!"

All hooked up, Connor steps off the platform and away he goes. The hum of the line vibrates in my ears as he speeds along. I watch until he's safely on the other platform, then let my eyes fall and fall to the canopy below.

"Don't look down," Grayson says lowly.

I do jump that time. When'd he come up next to me? My heart was already beating too quickly, but it accelerates even more with Grayson's close proximity. "Huh?"

"Don't look down." Maybe I was imagining things, wishful thinking probably, because now he's looking at the tree line behind us and speaking in a perfectly unattached voice "When you're out there, focus on the horizon. It'll make things easier."

I look at the horizon, processing his advice.

Before I can say anything, Fred says, "Who's first?" and Grayson steps forward quickly, like he can't get away from me fast enough. "I'll go."

It's like my body wants to follow him, or is left with too much wanting in his absence, because I sway a little when he goes. It doesn't help that I'm terrified of today's "fun activity." I grab the rail to steady myself.

Grayson and I were both kind of near the little opening to the Launch Pad. Fred unhooks the rope so Grayson can step out. I rub a thumb over the palm of my thick leather glove and watch as Fred gets things set up.

Just before he steps out, Grayson breaks out into a crooked grin. He doesn't just step off, he <u>launches</u> himself off the platform and goes flying down the line. My heart goes flying with him, for all sorts of reasons. Again, there's that humming as Grayson's carabiner slides down the steel cable.

I can't believe the way he flew off the platform. Several seconds later, he's on the next platform.

"Okay, next," Fred says.

"I'll go." One of the experienced guys approaches the rope eagerly.

"I don't know if I want to do this," Cotton Candy says behind me, but she's kind of laughing and I don't think she's really going to back out.

As I watch the guy get hooked up, I wish I'd gone. I'm getting more nervous the longer I stand here. I need to get this over with before I start thinking seriously about going back to the van.

The guy steps off the platform and slides down the line, which is humming again. I'm starting to get used to the sound. "Wooo hooo!" the guy hollers. Half way down he lets go of the line so he can spin around. Around and around on that little, tiny rope.

Uh, no. No thanks, for me.

My nerves rise as he gets closer to the other platform, hollering enthusiastically all the way. If I'm going to go next, it's almost time.

Bouncing slightly on the balls of my feet, I glance back and forth between the guy and Fred, who watches dispassionately as the guy reaches the opposite platform.

"Next."

"Me," I say urgently.

"Alright Chloe!" Bobby says behind me. I glance back and he gives me an enthusiastic thumbs up. I give him a shaky smile then look forward again. The butterflies are really loose in my chest now.

Fred unhooks the rope so I can cross through to that side of the platform. I get into position as I saw everyone else do. I watch as Fred hooks me up, making sure he really does it right. As if he wouldn't. But still.

And just like that, I'm attached to a three-hundred-foot steel cable dangling over a drop I'd rather not think too much about, if it's all the same to you. I almost look down, but then remember what Grayson said and look out at the view instead.

I grip the strap where it connects to the front of my harness, grab the cable above me with my gloved hand as instructed, and make myself put one foot in front of the other until there's nothing left but <u>nothing</u> and I'm suddenly zipping along.

I thought it'd feel like dropping on a roller coaster, but it doesn't. The wind's rushing past and I'm sailing down the line and it's... <u>amazing.</u>

There's a pretty, broad view to my right with its pine-topped hills sliding by. In the distance to my left, there's a few puffy white clouds. Their shadows stretch across the mountainside. I'm nearing the platform and start pulling down slightly with my gloved hand. Sure enough, it works! I start slowing down and then I'm there, headed for a padded wall directly in front of me. But my carabiner catches on the cable on the other side and Cute Connor slows me down just in time to stop before hitting the wall.

I'm back on my own two feet and grinning from ear to ear like an idiot.

"I did it!" I say to Cute Connor, who's smiling and getting me unhooked.

I look to Grayson, who's grinning at me too.

"I did it!" I say again. "That was fucking awesome!"

Grayson laughs and my heart soars and oh how I just want to run up to him and hug him. But I don't. Instead I settle for smiling at him and letting him smile back at me.

Connor steers me out of the way, to make room for the next person. The guy who went before me is leaning over the railing toward the group on the other platform, cupping his hands around his mouth. "Come on Victor, you chicken!" he hollers, then laughs.

I'm still reeling from my victory. See that big ol' steel cable right there? I just sailed my ass right down it and it was fantastic!

I look behind me but don't see another cable. "Hey, where's the next one?"

"Over there." Grayson points to a platform a ways off. "We take that trail right there."

I locate the dirt path leading into the forest. "Can we start walking now?"

"Ah, we have ourselves a convert." Cute Connor winks at me. "But you can't go on the next platform without me. You'll have to hang tight."

"I suppose." I grin, watching as the next person comes down.

We don't say much as we watch the rest of the group join us, one at a time. No one gets stuck, not even the newbies, though Cotton Candy screams the entire way. She's giggling by the time she gets back on her feet though and I can't help but laugh. Good for her for doing it.

A few people exit the platform and linger at the trailhead while the last people come down, but I stay. I want to watch everyone make it across. The middle-aged couple is last, but they do it and both seem like they enjoyed it. I hop off the platform and jog to the front of the group as we finally start down the trail.

I want to be first in line for the next go-round.

The next run is longer and gives us a fantastic view of a cliff face as we zip farther down the mountain. I was, in fact, first in line, but Grayson was one of the last. Bobby and his girl are one of the first ones too and I hang out with them a bit as we wait for the other members of our group. As the platform gets more crowded, however, I exit and wait at the trailhead with a few others.

And so it goes. We work our way from one zip line to the next, and I start to see why people seek out these kind of experiences. I try to practice good etiquette and let others go first, patiently (or not so patiently) waiting my turn. Grayson and I don't talk again until the second to the last run, when we both end up on the receiving platform together, before anyone else.

It's probably a good thing this hasn't happened too often, because even though Cute Connor isn't too far away, ready to receive the next person, I feel like Grayson and I are alone together. And that gets me all stirred up and wishing we could be <u>together</u>, in every sense of the word. I'm acutely aware of his presence, now that I'm not distracted by other people and breathtaking views.

I'm leaning on the front railing, my eyes on the cable. He's doing the same thing, though more than an arm's length away.

"I think your brother's coming next," he says, "but I'm not sure because his girlfriend was fighting him for the next place in line."

I groan. "She's not his girlfriend. Thank god."

"You don't like her?"

I glance at him and he's smiling at me knowingly. There's that cute dimple again. I smile too, my heart flip flopping.

I take a deep breath, my eyes back on the line. <u>That ship has sailed.</u> "It's not really my business." That's what I keep telling myself, anyway.

He nods, considering me. "So you're not feeling like you have to be his mom as much?"

I shrug. "I wish he had a mom, but he doesn't, and I'm not her, either. I guess even if Mom were still alive he'd be breaking away and making his own decisions."

"It's normal."

I nod.

"But it's hard?"

I nod. It's been the hardest thing for me to let go of during the past year, but I know it's better for both of us if I do. "It's getting better, though."

"Good for you, Chloe."

I look at him, drawn by the almost intimate tone in his voice. There's a brief moment when our eyes meet, and I feel that connection with him I felt all those months ago. I think my heart is going to burst. But it's so fast I don't know for sure that it even happened. Maybe it was just wishful fantasizing because he looks toward the line almost immediately.

"Here he comes." He nods his head.

Sure enough, there's Bobby. I look just in time to see him flip upside down and back up again. "Woooo hoooo!" he hollers, thrusting his arm in the air.

"Big dork," I say, laughing.

"Seems to run in the family," Grayson says smiling.

"Hey! I'm not a dork!"

He laughs. "It's okay. It's adorable on you." He's still not looking at me, but he's smiling.

So am I.

The last run is the best. We've worked our way down to the coast, and this line goes right over a little cove. Sailing down, the water stretches as far as the eye can see to my right. To my left is Swan Pointe, the resort up on the hill, and the beach dotted with people. I'm soaring above the ocean, getting closer and closer to the roaring waves as I near the final platform. Then, too soon, I'm back on my feet and my first zip lining journey is over.

I grin at Cute Connor and he gives me a wink. "Good job."

Only two riders remain, Grayson one among them. Most of the others have left the platform and are in various stages of removing their harnesses, or else heading up to the ridge where the van will pick us up to take us back to the resort.

I've taken off my helmet and rustled my hair with my fingers, but I'm not ready to go yet. I watch as the second-to-last rider comes down, Shane's aunt. She finishes her run with a big smile. Connor unhooks her and she climbs down the platform too.

I turn back to the line. It's still, waiting for the last rider. As am I. The surf is rhythmically pounding the shore, and the cool California breeze plays with my hair. I lean on the rail and put my chin in my hand.

Then I see him. Sailing over the cove. Larger than life, or so it seems to me. No matter where he's been today, my heart seems to want to pull in that direction. For just a moment, I indulge. I watch Grayson coming down the line toward me and pretend he's mine once more.

For just a moment.

Then he's on the platform, smiling and looking so handsome and thanking Connor amicably. I can't go up to him like I would if he were mine. I have to watch him from a distance, wishing I could close the last twenty feet between us.

He catches my eye and I almost forget to look away, but I manage it.

He's here with Sam. He shouldn't see me looking at him like that.

Chapter 11

We're the last ones to get free of our harnesses and end up walking toward the pick-up spot somewhat together. Connor and Fred are staying behind to pack up and say they'll meet us there.

The more Grayson and I walk in silence, the more uncomfortable the silence becomes. What happened in the past is looming between us again. I feel it. Or maybe it's just me. But now that we're really alone and can talk openly, I can't let it go.

"Grayson," I say softly. "I owe you an apology."

We continue on for several steps.

I glance at him. His face is unreadable. It's almost like he's trying to make sure I can't decipher his expression. Maybe he is.

"I shouldn't have left like that. I was... I was scared but..."

He finally looks at me, brow furrowed.

"It's no excuse and I know it." I look him in the eye, willing him to really see me. I want him to know I'm sincere. God, how I regret leaving him like I did. "It was childish of me. I'm really, really sorry."

We come to a stop, looking at one another.

"Scared of what?" Again that unreadable face.

For a moment I wonder if I imagined his intent with me that night. If I made something, where there wasn't anything. Part of me is so certain he felt things for me too, that night, but looking at him now I wonder. I do. <u>Was </u>it just me?

I take a deep breath. "I'd just broken up with Brad and you came along and it was..." <u>Amazing. Incredible. The best night of my entire life. </u>"It was just a little too much too soon for me."

He's listening, but his expression is still guarded.

I can't say that I blame him.

"Look, I..." I'm stumbling all over my words. I don't know if this is helping or making things worse or what I'm even trying to accomplish. "It wasn't you. You didn't do anything wrong."

"Why are you telling me this? What do you want me to do, Chloe?"

"Nothing. Nothing. I just wanted to... I don't know... try to explain myself. It's just sounding like a bunch of excuses, though, I know. I'm not trying to do that. And I'm not asking anything of you, obviously. I mean, you're with Sam. And Sam's great. I love her. I'm not trying to..." I sigh again. God, I just need to shut up now. "I'm sorry. That's all. What I did was terrible and I'm truly, truly sorry if I hurt you, Grayson."

He gives me the same impassive look he's been giving me the whole time. "You didn't."

I feel a little knocked back on my feet.

I'm not sure why his comment should make me feel badly. It's not that I wanted to have hurt him. "Oh," I say, trying to sound calm. "Well. I'm glad."

"Don't worry about it, Chloe." He starts walking again.

I fall in alongside him, too stunned to say a word.

We catch up to the others at the bottom of the hill. The shuttle van is just pulling up and there are a lot more people waiting to board than came with us earlier in the day. It looks like we're picking up a few resort guests from the beach too.

The van comes to a halt and the doors open. We load up. Bobby and Miss Cotton Candy sit near the front. I decide to keep my distance and sit in one of the benches closer to the back. Grayson comes down the aisle and slides in next to me.

I wish he hadn't.

Being in his presence for so long today is starting to take its toll. In spite of everything that's happened, even in spite of what he just said, I still want him. And not just physically, though there is that. It's <u>him.</u> Unlike the Night of Grayson, we've barely talked and haven't touched at all, but I'm as drawn to him now as I was that night.

In spite of everything, that connection I felt with him is happening again. Against my will.

Again.

The first night I fought it because I wasn't ready for another person in my life. I couldn't deal with being Chloe and somebody. Not then.

I could now though. I wouldn't hesitate to jump on board the Grayson train, if only things were different.

But things aren't different.

That train left the station the moment I walked out on him, and now he's with Sam. He's out of my reach in every sense of the word. So why can't I get my heart to stop reaching for him? Why am I tormenting myself?

And why did he sit by me? He's not talking and doesn't seem to want to talk. I don't know that I can handle talking right now anyway.

The shuttle idles in place, waiting for a large family hurrying up the hill to meet us.

They're hauling overstuffed beach bags and sun umbrellas. They climb on board, the bus swaying as they load in. The bus is nearly full though, so they spread out, squeezing in where they can. I assume the van will make the short trip to the resort and come back for the second group of zip liners that came up the mountain with us.

The father is the last man to board. He's a large gentleman and asks Grayson if the space next to him is taken.

"Go ahead," Grayson says, scooting over.

I quickly move over myself, trying to avoid coming into full contact with Grayson's body. I don't need that. Grayson, too, seems careful to give the man room without touching me.

This isn't a small man, though, and the seats aren't very long. There's more shuffling and scooting and before I know it the window is pressing against me on one side and Grayson's pressing against me on the other.

My heart is pounding. He's so close I can smell him. I remember that smell. His thigh is pressing hard against mine, all the way up to my hips. We're both wearing sleeveless tops, so our bare arms are touching. God, I remember this body.

"Sorry," Grayson murmurs.

The bus lurches into motion and our bodies move together.

I'm not looking out the window. I'm looking at the seat back in front of me and barely breathing. Grayson is immobile too, but maybe he's just pinned in. Like me. Maybe he's not happy about being pinned in.

But I like it.

I like it way too much.

To keep from putting my hand on the top of his thigh, I chant to myself: <u>He's here with Sam. He's here with Sam.</u>

Because that's the only thing holding me back. If it weren't for that, I'd risk everything my heart can hold just to put my hand on his knee.

As we head back to the resort, I realize I could move my forearm away and across my lap. That part of my arm doesn't <u>have</u> to be touching him like the rest of me does. But I don't move. My breathing is shallow and I'm tuned into every move his body makes

160

Then I realize he could move his forearm too, if he wanted to. He's not, but maybe the fact that our bodies are touching doesn't mean the same thing to him that it does to me.

I look down at his hand, resting on his knee. I take it all in: his tanned skin, the slightly raised veins, his short, clean nails. I remember the feel of that hand as it caressed my body: along my waist, over my breasts, up the inside of my thighs.

I look sharply out the window. I have to stop. I have to stop thinking like this.

But I do not move and my heart continues to pound.

We pull up to the hotel and the bus comes to a stop.

It's almost over. This moment with Grayson. And I don't want it to be.

The doors open and people start to climb off. I'm still not moving. The man at the end of our bench heaves himself up and shuffles down the aisle.

Grayson does not move. Not one inch.

I slowly look at him, then he slides out and away and my body is cold where Grayson used to be.

Isabella's family provided a "casual dinner" in one of the resort's banquet halls tonight. The tables were exquisitely decorated and the buffet was overflowing with food. My favorite was the bacon-wrapped dates (I went back for more twice), but the eating seems more or less done now.

Isabella and Shane are over at a table with three sets of grandparents. I've been sharing a table with Bobby, Ashley, a couple of Isabella's young cousins from Texas (all-American girls who don't look related to her one whit), and of course Sam and Grayson.

This is how it's gone down.

Sam is the sexy, charming, endearing little flirt she's always been. Grayson is gorgeous, gracious, and enjoying the evening, so far as I can tell. He laughs at Sam's stories and quips—like we all do—and I look at the two of them as little as humanly possible.

Not looking at him doesn't stop me from entertaining my little fantasies. This evening, I've imagined all sorts of ways Grayson and I could end up together after all. Maybe Sam won't care. She's not in love with him and I did have him first.

Not that Grayson wants me.

He's over there right now, talking to Bobby and laughing and looking perfectly charming. Sam's smiling too. They both look happy enough to me. Of course, anyone looking at me might think the same thing. I'm putting up a pretty good act. I've even entertained the table with my Christmas tree story.

In fact, anyone who didn't know better would look at our little group and think there couldn't be anything wrong with the world at all.

That just shows what any of us knows, doesn't it?

Chapter 12

After a night's rest, I'm freshly resolved to keep it together and enjoy the day. It's what a strong, independent woman would do. Right?

Around eleven o'clock in the morning, the entire crew of relatives and friends who've come to enjoy the early celebrations for Shane and Isabella's wedding are down at the docks. We're all heading for the resort's luxurious 400-foot yacht, which her parents have chartered for the entire day. We'll be taking a leisurely tour down the coast and back, and cap off the evening with dinner on board.

I tell you what, those people who aren't arriving for the wedding until Saturday are missing out. The Golden Pearl is a massive vessel, gleaming in the California sun. I've been told it has three decks, two pools, and enough liquor to fuel a frat party for a month.

I don't know how much partying will be going on, what with all the elderly-type guests who'll be aboard, but I could use a shot of something, that's for damned sure. I'm walking along the dock, my day bag hitched over my shoulder, and Sam and Grayson are walking right in front of me. He's carrying both their bags, but she has one arm hooked into the crook of his arm.

Look, I've seen Sam like this with countless guys. I'm no more concerned that she's getting attached to him than I was two days ago.

It's just that it's, you know, Grayson. God.

But I'm determined to keep my emotions in check. I have to. I'm the one who made this decision after all. I need to suck it up and deal with it. Plus, I've been looking forward to the day's activity for months. I mean, how often does a person like me get to spend the day on board a fucking yacht? So I keep telling myself not to pay attention to Sam and Grayson and instead focus on how fun it will be to get on board and check things out.

Grayson says something funny and Sam rewards him with one of her lighthearted laughs, the kind that makes everyone around her smile too.

I take a deep breath. I can do this.

There's something like sixty of us making our way to the <u>Golden Pearl,</u> but Sam, Grayson, Ashley and I are near the rear. It's too bad Bobby had to go back home last night. We tried to get him to call in sick to work this morning, but he wouldn't do it. In some ways, he's more responsible than I am. I totally would've done it.

As the front of the massive wedding party reaches the gangway and starts to board, I glance toward the parking lot, looking for Jack's truck.

"Where is he?" I ask Sam.

He's driving in from Rosebrook this morning to join us and she's been in regular contact with him. (Of course, she's pretty much always in regular contact with him.) Isabella and Shane are waiting in the parking lot so they can lead him to the ship once he gets here, but I can see they're still over there waiting.

Sam pulls her phone out and sends him a text. "He should be here any—"

"There he is!" I say, seeing his truck pull into the parking lot at last. Oh hell, I should've just waited in the parking lot with Isabella. I haven't seen Jack since I moved to Boise and the sight of his truck has me heading back to greet him.

Ashley, Sam, and Grayson trail after me, but as Jack pulls into a parking spot and climbs out, I pick up the pace. I didn't realize how much I've missed my friend until I see his face. Shane and Isabella are greeting him. Jack's wearing that big goofy grin I love so much, and clapping Shane on the back. He gives Isabella a perfectly tame hug—just like a regular person would do—but smiles at her warmly and she smiles back up at him.

Once Isabella and Shane got together, I noticed Jack kind of adjusted his shows of physical affection toward her, like he didn't want to step on Shane's turf or something. But the rest of us girls are under no such restrictions.

As I hurry toward them, Jack sees me and hollers out enthusiastically, "Chloe! Baby!"

I drop my bag and throw my arms around him as he picks me up into a great, big Jack hug. "Hey Jack!" I hang on tighter as he spins me in circles. "Ahhhh!" By the time he sets me down I'm laughing and hanging on to him, slightly dizzy.

Ashley, Sam, and Grayson are just coming up to us. Grayson is watching the scene unfold with the kind of fascination most guys have when they first see Jack with his little harem.

"Gee, did you miss me?" I tease.

"Hell, yes." He keeps his arm around my shoulder as he pulls Ashley into a half hug and kisses her on the cheek. Since she and Sam both live in Rosebrook, they get to see Jack all the time. "Why the fuck did you move to Boise?" he asks me.

Grayson's eyebrows shoot up at this piece of information. I haven't mentioned my move to him and Sam must not have said anything either. Why would she?

"I wanted to start my blog," I answer evasively.

"It's not like you couldn't have started a blog when you were in Swan Pointe." Jack's grinning, but I can hear the serious tone in his voice. Sam has mentioned he thinks I need to move back "home" where I belong.

I glance uncomfortably at Grayson again. "I know."

Moving to Boise was complicated, and it wasn't the job itself that lured me. Though I'm making a tiny bit more money, the company is massive, so I'm a member of one of their many 'teams.' I feel like one little cog in a long line of cogs. But still, I had reasons for accepting that job offer. Taking that kind of leap <u>did</u> give me the courage I needed to really work on my blog, but of course it was also a way to escape the Temptation of Grayson. I knew if I stayed in Swan Pointe, it would only be a matter of time before I showed up on his doorstep.

Sam comes up to greet him. Still keeping one arm around me (I'm not in much of a hurry to let go of my friend either), Jack hooks his other arm around Sam's neck and puts his forehead to hers, holding her eyes with a mock, stern look.

"Hey Shorty," he says, "you took the last of my Turtle brownies."

"My Turtle brownies." She lightly slaps him on the stomach. "I'm the one who made them."

She ducks out from under Jack's arm and returns to Grayson's side, smiling. "Grayson, this is Jack. Jack, Grayson. He's my date for the week."

"Hey man, nice to meet you." Jack shakes hands amicably.

"You, too," Grayson says smiling, but he's still trying to figure everything out. I can tell.

"Do you have a bag?" Isabella asks.

"Yeah, in the back."

He kisses the top of my head and squeezes my shoulders before finally releasing me. I'm feeling more buoyant, now that Jack's here. Maybe today won't be so bad after all.

As Jack heads to the back of his truck, Sam leaves Grayson's side and climbs into Jack's cab. Her head disappears as she, apparently, starts looking in his glove box.

"What are you looking for?" Jack calls up to her.

"My CD."

"It's in the player." He hefts his duffle bag onto his shoulder.

"I'm going to put it in your suitcase so you don't forget," she says, reappearing. "You can give it to me when we get back to the hotel."

Grayson has a weird look on his face. I'll admit, it kills me to think he might be jealous of Jack, but I don't really want him to suffer needlessly. Because I'm a sucker like that.

I step next to him, trying to ignore what being this close to his body does to me. I say quietly, "Don't worry. Jack's not into Sam or anything."

Grayson gives me a look I can't quite read.

"He's a friend," I say. "That's it."

"What about... anyone else?" he asks, returning his attention to Sam, who's scooting back out of Jack's truck. "Is Jack into Ashley or... you?"

His question gives me pause. If I didn't know better, I'd think Grayson was jealous about <u>me.</u>

Is he?

No, I'm being stupid. I didn't just close that door, I blew it into oblivion. And Grayson's given every indication he's not interested in opening it again. Plus there's always the Not Insignificant Fact that he's here with <u>Sam.</u>

"No, Jack's harmless," I say. "He's practically an honorary Firework Girl."

Jack locks up his truck and we head toward the yacht. Sam is back with Grayson and I gratefully stick close to Jack, who has his arm draped over my shoulder again. "Which one is it?" He's scanning the ships moored at the docks.

I point to the <u>Golden Pearl</u>. "That big white one at the end."

"<u>That</u> one? Damn, Isabella, you've been holding out on us. That's the biggest one here!"

"This was all my mother's doing." Isabella throws her hands in the air as if to say, <u>Don't blame me</u>. We all know Isabella's mother isn't much prone to extravagances, except where her daughter is concerned. And when she found out her only child was getting married? Well, clearly she's pulled out all the stops.

"You're a good daughter to accommodate her," Jack says, "and we're such good friends to go along with it. I mean, not many people would be willing to put up with a whole day of <u>yachting</u>, but for <u>you</u> honey..."

Isabella laughs. "I'm actually kind of excited, too. Does that make me shallow?"

"Yep," Sam says, "but you're in good company. We'll all be good and shallow with you. I just want to know if I'm supposed to wear heels with my bikini or something."

"Your diamond-studded bikini," I add.

"Ah darn," she says, "I accidentally left it in the limo."

"Actually," Shane says, "I think Ashley's going to be more excited than anyone."

"Me?" Ashley says in surprise. "Why me?"

Shane and Isabella are walking arm in arm and smile at each other. "You'll see," Isabella says.

We make it to the docks and up the gangplank at last. As we board the <u>Golden Pearl,</u> we're wrapped in the intoxicating spell of extravagant wealth. The rest of the group is on deck and has apparently been waiting for us so that the porters, in their smart little uniforms, can take everyone on a tour.

I don't even bother trying not to gawk as we're led through exquisite lounge rooms, a fully-equipped kitchen, and the huge dining hall with overflow onto a private dining deck. We peek into luxurious state rooms, admire the game room complete with three pool tables, and drool over the theatre with plush bucket seats.

"Good god," Sam says. "Who lives like this?"

"We do, baby," Jack says, "for the next eight hours."

"They'll have to drag my ass off this boat kicking and screaming," she says. "Do you think I could stow away in a closet or something?"

"You could stow away in a bottle, Shorty."

"Shut up, Jack."

174

The main level features the largest of the yacht's two pools, situated on the huge deck at the bow. There's a sizeable Jacuzzi as well. Inside is a massive lounge. Here we're greeted with a large buffet of croissant sandwiches, paninis, fruit, antipasto platters, and desserts. Apparently we'll be taking our plates to the deck so we can eat lunch while enjoying the view during departure. This would sort of be considered "casual dining" were it not for the fact that we're aboard a freaking yacht.

While Jack eyes the desserts eagerly, we finally discover what Ashley has to be excited about. On the far side of the room is a full-sized, grand piano.

"Is that a Fazioli?" Ashley breathes, breaking from the group and rushing up to it. Gaping at it, she runs one hand over the sleek wood and checks out the imprint on the front. "This is a Fazioli!" She looks back at us with her mouth hanging open.

"Enjoy," Isabella says, smiling.

Ashley sinks onto the bench, her eyes drinking in the piano as if she's died and gone to heaven.

"And that's the last we'll see of her," I say, grinning.

"I guess that's a pretty good piano, eh?" Sam says.

"Ranks right up there, from what I understand," Shane answers.

Before Ashley can start playing, however, the captain arrives to introduce himself and welcome us. We're assured the crew is there to make us comfortable and we're not to hesitate if we need anything at all.

Jack has subtly shuffled himself closer to the food tables. He's waiting for the first polite opportunity to strike, I know. Actually, the way he's eyeing the mini tarts, I'm not sure he'll make it that long.

At last, we're released from the formality of the tour, the captain departs, Jack dives for a tart, and Ashley starts playing. As the first notes of her song fill the room, a temporary silence falls over the crowd. A few people wander over, drawn by her magic. Only Ashley could do justice to the grandeur of our surroundings. At the conclusion of the piece, she nods graciously to their astonished compliments and starts another song.

I smile. This place is truly heavenly. What's not to love about it?

As I turn toward the food tables, Sam reminds me. I'm just in time to see her go up on tip toe and plant a firm kiss on Grayson. I look away and abruptly head for—no place in particular, it turns out—with the image of them kissing still burning into my eyes.

Turns out heaven is plenty large enough to hold a little piece of hell.

Chapter 13

Our journey down the coast is truly magnificent, or would be if I weren't feeling increasingly hemmed in by the fact that I'm here with Sam and Grayson. In spite of the size of this thing, I can't seem to escape them. And I've tried. But no matter where I go, someone draws me back to the group.

Jack was the latest culprit. He found me lounging on one of the upper deck chairs and decided that wouldn't do at all. After luring me to the deck of the main pool to join the others, he unceremoniously picked me up and threw me into the deep end.

It was a welcome diversion, as it turns out. There we all were—the Firework Girls, Jack, Shane, and Grayson—dunking, splashing, and generally messing around, and I forgot for a while to be upset. In fact, I rather enjoyed being so close to Grayson in a suit.

Hottest guy present, hands down.

But when the rowdiness hit a lull and Sam, in her cute little string bikini, wrapped her arms around Grayson's neck with that flirty look she gets, I couldn't stay. Under pretense of getting a drink from the poolside bar, I extricated myself from the scene and ended up face-down on a lounge, sunbathing.

That's where I'm at right now. I figure if I'm within sight of the group maybe they'll stop reeling me back in. I really, really don't want to do this anymore.

Every time they all erupt in laughter, it's Grayson's laugh that makes my heart ache.

How did I get myself into this mess?

Another twenty minutes or so go by. I flip to my back and watch as the group slowly makes their way to the shallow end, apparently on their way out of the pool.

Sam and Grayson exit first, heading for the towel rack next to me. Of course. Of all the lounges I could've parked myself on, why did I choose this one?

I inwardly sigh, but outwardly plaster on a smile. They're both grinning and start drying off. We hear Ashley squeal and look in time to see Jack has sneak attacked her and dunked her under the water.

"I'm convinced Jack is in love with one of you," Grayson says as Jack bounds up the steps, laughing, "but hell if I know which one."

"I'm his favorite," I say automatically, retreating to an old joke.

"You wish," Sam says.

"Girls, girls," Jack says, drawing near with an impish grin on his face. "There's plenty of me to go around." He raises both arms and flexes his muscles dramatically. "Oh yeah. Look at those biceps. Try not to swoon, fair ladies."

Sam throws a towel at him but he catches it deftly. "Get over thyself."

He winks at her and throws the towel over his head, rubbing vigorously. Ashley, Isabella, and Shane come up and grab their own towels.

"Oooh Chloe," Sam says, eyeing a guy across the pool and sinking down next to me. "That's the one right there."

"The one for what?"

"Your date for the reception. He's perfect for you."

I glance at Grayson, who meets my eye then looks away. "No thanks," I say.

"Come on," Sam says, "he's <u>so</u> cute."

I take a better look at the target. He's in red swim trunks and lying on a lounge across the pool from us. "I guess."

"Are you blind? He's completely f—"

"Do <u>not</u> finish that sentence."

I glance at Grayson. He looks irritated. Maybe he doesn't like Sam drooling over the cute guy over there.

"Come on, Chloe," Sam continues. "I say we go over there and get you in his line of sight. I'll be your wing man."

"Ugh. Pick on Ashley for once, would you?"

"Good luck with that," Isabella says smiling.

"Ashley and I have an understanding," Sam says dismissively, waving her hand.

"You have an understanding with Sam?" I say to Ashley. "How do I get me one of those?"

Ashley's face is impassive and she's not quite meeting my eyes. It occurs to me just how little I've seen Ashley dating over the years. She's gone on dates, yes, but not many, and she's never been serious about anyone. She claims she doesn't have time for relationships, what with all of her practicing, but she's never had difficulties making time to hang with us.

Ashley shrugs and says lightly, "A little bribing and threatening gets you a long way with Sam."

"That's true," Grayson pipes in.

I look at him sharply, but he's drying off, not looking at me.

"Oh come on," Sam says. "I'm just trying to help. You're my friend. I can see you need some spanky hot sex."

Out of the corner of my eye, I see Grayson glance at me, but I'm looking Sam directly in the eyes. "Cut. It. Out."

She tilts her head at me and I see she's finally gotten the message. "Oh fine," she says easily. "I'll just let you admire him from afar." She winks at me and pats my arm, then stands and goes to Grayson.

"As for <u>you</u> mister." She snakes her arm around Grayson's waist. "I have something I want to show you."

My heart drops and I look away to the pool. My skin is crawling. Throughout the day, I've seen a few couples sneaking into the state rooms. I wonder if that's where Sam and Grayson are heading.

I don't want to know. I don't want to know. I don't want to know.

"We're going to go play pool," Isabella says to me, as Sam and Grayson disappear inside. "Want to join us?"

"<u>They're</u> going to play pool," Ashley says. "I'm getting my tail back to that piano."

"Actually, I think I'm going to get cleaned up." I stand, not looking at anyone.

"Dinner's not for a while," Shane says. "You have time."

"And maybe take a nap," I add.

"Okay," Isabella says with a wave. "We'll catch you later."

I force myself to smile as they leave. I head to the lower level and the cabin with several of our bags in it, feeling sick to my stomach the whole way.

Once I'm showered, changed, and done with my makeup, I'm a little more in control. But just a little.

I follow the sound of Ashley's music to the main lounge. She's still in her shorts and tank, not yet changed for dinner. I pick an empty spot on the couch nearest her and sink onto it, letting the comforting lilt of the music wash over me. I could listen to Ashley play all day.

She wraps up one song and flows easily into the next. This one is sort of haunting and pulls out all my longing for Grayson. Or maybe any song would do that right now. I was longing for him before I even sat down. Heart aching, I sink lower on the couch and let my head rest on the back, watching her. She catches my eye and gives me a questioning glance. I can't bring myself to smile or pretend.

As she finishes the number, an older couple comes over and requests a song. She rarely refuses requests, but she graciously backs out of this one, eyeing me the whole time.

They finally leave and she comes over and sits next to me. "So," she says gently, "how are you handling the thing with Grayson?"

I sigh. I don't even know where to begin.

"That good, huh?"

I shrug. "It doesn't really matter. It's too late to tell Sam now." It'd be even worse.

"Do you wish you'd said something?"

"I don't know. No. It still wouldn't have been fair. To either one of them."

Ashley gives me an appraising look. "Why do I get the feeling," she says slowly, "that you're not telling me something?"

"Probably because I'm not telling you something."

She sinks low and lays her head on the back of the couch too, waiting. My heart starts pounding in anticipation of my impending confession.

"I..." How do I say this? I lower my voice and try again. "I kind of still have feelings for Grayson."

Her eyebrows raise.

"Actually, that's not quite right, either," I continue.

Ashley furrows her brows at me. I sit up slightly and look around to make sure Sam and Grayson are nowhere in sight. I settle back and turn back to Ashley.

"I sort of fell in love with Grayson that night," I say lowly.

"What?!"

"Shhh!" I look around again. The scene hasn't changed.

"How could you fall in love with him?" she whispers urgently.

"I don't know," I say miserably.

"I thought you said it was just a one-night stand."

"It was one night, but it wasn't a one-night stand." That's never felt like the right phrase for what happened between us. It wasn't a one-night stand at all. It was the Night of Grayson, and those are two completely different things.

I proceed to tell Ashley what happened— as best as I can explain what I thought I felt between us—along with what happened the next morning. A few times tears start to rise up, but I push them back down. I can't cry over Grayson. Especially now.

When I'm finished, Ashley says, "Oh, sweetie."

I shrug miserably. What's to be done?

"Okay," she says gently, "you have to tell Sam."

"What? No!"

"She has to know."

"Why? What difference does it make? I ran out on him. It's not like there's any chance of us getting back together."

"But... this has to be killing you. Sam wouldn't want to put you through that."

"It's—" I sigh. "Look, I've thought about all this a hundred times. But how crappy would it be for me to pull the rug out from underneath them?"

Ashley frowns, not quite convinced.

"I can't do that to him again and... yeah it sucks that he's here with Sam but it's not like that's going to last forever. Plus it's Isabella's wedding and..." I hesitate before putting voice to a relatively new fear, "what if Sam gets mad?"

"Why would she get mad?"

"You remember what happened with Loni."

Ashley pauses. I can see by the hesitation on her face that she does remember Loni.

Loni was Isabella's roommate freshman year, but we all hung out together and got pretty close. Sam cut her off after Loni slept with Sam's ex. Loni thought Sam wouldn't care because he was practically a one-night stand, but Sam was livid. She just couldn't get over the fact that Loni would sleep with the same guy she slept with. The rest of us tried to patch things over, but it was just over between them after that.

"This is different, though," Ashley says.

"But is <u>Sam</u> going to think it's different? Especially when I could've said something right away but didn't?"

"I don't know. I think she would. Probably."

Yeah, that's about how certain I feel about it. "Look, it doesn't matter anyway.

Telling Sam doesn't change anything and I don't want to risk upsetting the cart in the middle of Isabella's wedding week. There's just no point. I can't be with Grayson anyway and he'll be out of her life too, soon enough. I just need to get through this and then it'll be over."

Ashley sighs. "I guess, but God, honey. This sucks."

I nod. "Yeah. It helps to talk about it, though. Thanks for listening."

Ashley gives me a sympathetic smile.

I do feel a little better. I just need to get through the rest of the week. In three days I'll be on a plane back to Boise and life can go back to normal.

I try to ignore the ache that thought creates, while Ashley returns to the piano to play me my favorite song.

Chapter 14

About an hour later, Ashley leaves to get ready for dinner and I go to the upper deck just in time to see the sun sink into the water. The yacht is on its way back to the resort, so I circle around to the other side to watch the twinkling lights of the little town on the coast. I'm not even sure what town it is. We're still a couple hours from docking, I think, but we've been traveling at such a leisurely pace I don't really know how far we'd gone before we turned around to head back.

I hope dinner isn't assigned seating, or if it is, I hope I'm far away from Sam and Grayson. It's easier to handle everything when they're not right in my face. Though, in spite of all my avoidance maneuvering, this evening still hasn't been easy at all.

Then I hear his voice. "Hey."

I spin to see him coming along the promenade deck. He's wearing slacks and a nice button-down shirt and is back to looking impossibly handsome. He's alone—and giving me a rather serious expression—but I still glance around for her. "Where's Sam?"

"Getting ready."

He comes up next to me and leans on the rail, turning his attention to the shoreline.

I go back to the view as well. I should leave. But I don't.

We stand there in silence for a few moments, the town sliding by in front of us. Without moving my head, I glance down at his hands. They're clasped loosely together. I want to run my fingers over them.

"How's your channel going?" I finally ask, unable to bear being so close to him without either kissing him or speaking. Since the first isn't really an option...

"Pretty good."

I guess that's all I'm going to get. I nod. "That's good," I say awkwardly. I really, really should go, but I like being here with him.

"When did you move to Boise?" he asks.

"About..." <u>Six days after I met you,</u> "...nine months ago."

I can't help but look at him when I say it. He's watching the shoreline, but gets a strange expression on his face. I don't say that I spent all six of those days fighting the urge to go to his house and beg him to forgive me. I swear, the job offer in Boise was the only thing that saved me.

Of course, at this exact moment I'm not so sure leaving Grayson was salvation, exactly. But when I think back to where I was at that time, and when I think about how much I've grown as a person over the last nine months, I still know in my heart the timing for Grayson wasn't just wrong, it was <u>terrible.</u>

I look away to the coast in frustration. Sometimes life just sucks.

"Did you know you were moving when we..." he lets it trail away.

I shake my head. "No."

There's a pause, then he says quietly, "I haven't said anything to Sam about... you know."

192

The Night of Grayson. Yes, I know. "I figured that. She'd definitely say something to me about it if she knew."

My tone must reveal my dread at the idea of her knowing, because he says, "Well, she couldn't be mad at you for it."

I look at him. Maybe. Maybe not. He doesn't know Sam like I do. She's fiercely loyal to her friends, but if she thinks you've betrayed her...

"You haven't done anything wrong," he continues. "Especially because you were..." He stops abruptly.

He isn't finishing his sentence, so I do it for him. "First. I know." I'm irritated and having a hard time hiding it. The thought of Grayson and Sam together...

"Well, look, I just wanted to tell you that I accept," he says. I look at him again. "Your apology, I mean. I don't think I said that yesterday."

I blink at him, but he's still just studying the shoreline. "I understand how that night might have been a little... overwhelming." He glances at me tentatively. "It was pretty intense, I know."

I nod. Intense. Yeah. That's one word for it.

"It's for the best, though. It only proved the Rule is a good thing."

My skin is starting to crawl again. I'm not sure why. "The 'not till you're thirty' rule?"

"Because otherwise you're too young and do stupid things, right? I mean..." his eyes are still fixed on the shoreline. "I was being stupid. Love at first sight isn't real. People who are too young mistake infatuation for love all the time."

I look at him sharply. Love at first sight? Had he felt that too? Or is he saying he only thought it was love, but it... wasn't?

"But it's for the best," he says firmly, nodding. "It woke me up and reminded me I need to stick to the Rule. No matter what. I can't end up like my parents. I don't want that. When I marry, I want it to last, but not out of sheer stubbornness. I want to be like those old couples you see, still holding hands and making each other laugh. I'm willing to wait for that. I just..."

He glances at me, then away again.

"I don't want to make a mistake. You made me even more determined not to break the Rule. So, it was a good thing. That way."

My heart is pounding with dread. The dinner bell starts ringing and I startle.

"It was for the best," he says again, shrugging. "Don't feel guilty." Still without looking at me, he pats me on the shoulder and walks away.

The bell is still ringing. I follow him in a sort of haze. As we join the crowds slowly flowing toward the dining room, my pace slows and we get separated.

It's over with Grayson. I've been saying it for months. I've been saying it all week. And I'm the one who ended it. But I didn't realize until just this moment that I only believed it in my mind.

Now my heart's catching up to things.

I killed it forever. I really, really did.

Somewhere inside of me I must have thought I still had a chance, because the weight of the realization that I have no chance is flattening me. The tears are building from somewhere deep inside me. I think I'm going to cry right here and now.

I hold it in. I can't cry here. I can't cry now.

Numbly, I float into the dining room. I check the tags, find mine, and sit down. He's directly across from me and Sam comes in and sits to his left. Ashley sits to my right. All these people sit down and Isabella's father stands and welcomes us and the porters start serving and all I can think is this:

It really is over.

I look at Grayson, not quite realizing he's looking at me too and I should look away. You know, to be proper or whatever the hell. But all I can do is look at him and realize he's not mine and never will be mine and I don't know if I can handle that.

Sam leans into him, wearing that carefree smile of hers. "Oh Grayson, I have to tell you the funniest story."

I look at her, furrowing my brows. I'm trying to remember why Sam gets to be the one to tell him funny stories. How the hell did this happen?

Isn't Grayson supposed to be mine? But he's not. And he's glad about it.

196

He thinks it's for the best.

"You okay, Chloe?" Sam asks me. "You're not looking well."

"I'm fine," I answer automatically. "I have a headache."

I'm still looking at Grayson and he's looking right back at me. How could he have said that? That night meant everything to me, and he's just glad it's over.

"Why don't you go lie down," Sam says. "That big State room is on this deck. Why don't you go to that one?"

I must not look good because everyone's watching at me with concern. I manage to smile—who knew I was so good at fake smiling when I only want to be real crying—and say, "I'm alright. Thank you, though."

I don't want to make a scene and besides, if I leave this table, I really will be crying and now is not the time.

I try to steel myself. I need to get it together. I focus on my plate, noticing what's in front of me for the first time. Some sort of creamy soup. It's orange. What the fuck is this?

Tears are dangerously close to the surface. Everyone's starting to eat, so I mechanically dip my spoon in my bowl.

Sam says something about how good the soup is. "Isn't it amazing?"

She must have asked Grayson—I wouldn't know because I'm not looking—because he says, "It is."

That's all he says, but his voice pierces me to the very core.

I stand abruptly, my chair scraping against the floor. "I'm really not feeling well," I say to no one in particular. "I think I will go lie down. I'm sorry."

Chapter 15

There's only the one State room on this level, the master, and I go straight to it. By the time I'm in the room and heading for the bed, my vision is too blurry to appreciate the view from the wall of windows facing the sea.

I collapse on the bed and curl on my side, helpless to stop the sobs tearing out of me. Nine months of not crying over Grayson is coming back to me with a vengeance. I should've just let myself cry over him instead of trying to be strong because then I wouldn't be falling apart now. Now, at the most inopportune time. As a reward for my stubbornness, I not only get to cry nine months of tears in one fell swoop, I get to feel like an idiot for running out of dinner.

As hard as I've tried not to be a hopeless, fucked up mess, I've managed to pull it off anyway.

When Brad ran out on me a year ago, I thought I knew what heartbreak was.

I was wrong.

I'm not sure how long it's been. My tears have dried up and I'm resting in that post-cry numbness. Grateful for the reprieve, I'm lying on the bed and staring at the windows. It's dark outside, so the room is reflected back at me. I hear the lulling of the ship's engines humming through the floor.

There's a quiet knock and the door behind me cracks open. I knew it would only be a matter of time before Ashley or Jack or someone came to check on me. Prepared for this eventuality, I've already wiped my face and have my headache excuse at the ready. I'm about to sit up and rejoin the world like a normal human, when the reflection in the glass shows me who it is.

Grayson steps in, glances at me lying on the bed, and silently closes the door behind him.

I'm frozen. My heart pounds painfully in my chest. As he quietly makes his way around the corner of the bed, I turn slightly to look at him full on. The man I love.

"If you've come to tell me that night meant nothing to you," I say, "then don't."

He stops short, staring at me.

"Seriously, Grayson. I can't listen to that again, okay? Just..." I look back to the glass. "Go away."

He hovers there for a moment. I can't stand him seeing me like this. Instead of going away like I need him to, he comes up and sits on the edge of the bed, right next to me.

I turn to him, ready to be firm.

I don't remember what I was going to say, though, because I'm struck by the pained expression on his face.

"I lied to you, Chloe." There's a quiet kind of agony in his voice.

I furrow my brows and open my mouth to speak, but he pushes ahead.

"I've been telling myself you weren't who I thought, because the person I thought you were wouldn't just walk out like that."

His words cut me to the quick. I start to sit up, wanting to apologize again, but he rushes on.

"I thought it proved everything. You know? It proved that it was stupid to think I love you. I don't even know you. It makes no sense. You can't really fall in love like that. I know that. But still you came along and... and you fucked me all up, Chloe... because I <u>did</u> fall in love with you and I'm <u>still</u> in love with you and I know that makes no sense but it's true."

My heart is pounding. I don't think I'm breathing.

His hands cup my face and my hands grip his arms in desperation. The tears start flowing freely again. Some sort of knot has come undone in my heart.

"I haven't been able to stop thinking about you," he says thickly. "Not for a single day. Please," he breathes, "tell me it wasn't just me."

He looks at me desperately and my heart is breaking wide open with relief and desire and agony. I wish I could turn back time and stay. Just <u>stay.</u> "It wasn't just you," I whisper. "It wasn't."

He exhales sharply.

"I'm so sorry for leaving you like that, Grayson. It was too soon and you were just <u>so much.</u>"

Still looking in pain, he rubs my tears off first one cheek, then the other. "I came on too strong. I know it. I couldn't help it. Everything about you had me breaking every rule in the book. The more we talked and the more we were together, the more I thought, 'I can't let this one go.' It was the most impulsive, all-in feeling I've ever had. The fact that it was supposed to be your wedding night and it had only been a few months since you ended this really long relationship... those alarm bells were going off in the back of my head and I just ignored them. Because that's what people do and that's when they get in trouble. That's why I had the Rule. But that night I didn't care and God help me I still don't. But when I came out and you were gone." Tears are running down my cheeks. "Just... gone. No note. Not a word."

"I'm so sorry."

"I thought it meant nothing to you."

"It meant <u>everything</u> to me. You had me. You had me. I ran because I was so, so scared of what that meant. I'm sorry I wasn't ready then. I wish I could go back—"

But I can't finish because he leans in and kisses me hard.

My heart stops and for half a second I'm frozen, inside and out. Everything I thought was true about our situation has been turned completely on its head. All my mind can think now is, <u>He's mine. He's mine.</u>

My heart begins to pound and I throw my arms around his neck and kiss him back. Our mouths open to each other and our tongues search each other frantically. My whimpers float in my ears. Now that I have him in my arms I'm terrified to let go.

He pulls back slightly, one hand on my face. "I tried to make myself move on." He looks positively tortured. "But I've just been going through the motions." His breath is shaky. "It didn't help because even before I got here, everything around me was <u>you.</u> All I want…" his voice is husky, his hot breath on my lips, "is to be with you. It's all I've wanted since the day I met you."

I kiss him again. I kiss him with a depth of passion and love I didn't know it was possible to feel. I want him. I want this man. And he wants me too. As I fall into his kiss and his embrace, it's all I can think about. All I'm aware of.

Mad with longing, I taste him deeply and clutch him to me. I can't let go. I can't do it. I can't lose him again. He holds me fiercely too, our tongues hungry for each other.

He leans me back and falls on top of me, holding me tight. I wrap myself around him, needing him. My legs tighten around his waist. His hands go into my hair. I can't get enough.

<u>Wait,</u> a voice in the back of my head whispers.

We angle our hips toward one another and his hard shaft digs against me. I feel his desire for me, there and everywhere. I can't touch him enough or hold him tightly enough. My whole heart and body has caught fire.

Wait.

He kisses my neck hungrily, pulling my shirt off my shoulder and frantically working his way along my bare skin. Panting, I arch my head back, wanting more of him. His hand reaches underneath my top and squeezes my breast. With his hardness against me, I squeeze my legs tighter, pressing into him.

Wait. Sam.

And then I realize what I'm doing. And where I am. And who else is on this ship with me. And I'm mortified.

I'm so in the grips of wanting him I don't even pause. I dip my mouth toward his, asking for him, and he returns to me, kissing me eagerly.

But now that I've remembered, I can't unremember. My thoughts catch up with my body and I pull back slightly.

"Wait", I say weakly, not meaning it like I should.

Then I'm kissing him with even more urgency because I know I have to stop and I don't want to. God, he's right here in my arms and I'm in his. I'm nearly dizzy with the relief of holding him again.

But Sam.

She would definitely, definitely not be okay with this.

Then I really and truly am mortified and break away, catching his eyes with mine.

"Oh god," I say. "Sam."

He blinks at me. "No, honey, I don't love Sam. That's what I was trying to tell you. It's not like that—"

I shake my head. He doesn't understand. I don't even know what to do with what he just said. I already know he doesn't love Sam. That's not the point. "I love Sam."

He pulls back a bit and looks at me.

"Oh God, what am I doing? She's my friend. I can't—"

The door knob rattles and our eyes fly wide. He scrambles off as the door swings open. He's still leaning over me slightly and I'm still yanking my shirt back onto my shoulder when Jack clears the door, takes one look at us, and halts.

My hands fly to my eyes.

As if I could hide from this.

I'm only like that for a second, but that second feels like a lifetime. My body is throbbing with horror.

"What the fuck?" Jack says softly.

I drop my hands and look at him. His eyes are darting back and forth between us. He doesn't look shocked. At least, he doesn't just look shocked. Jack looks pissed.

I turn away and swing my feet over the edge of the bed. I grip the edge of the mattress with both hands.

I glance at Grayson. I can't begin to guess what he's thinking. His face is a mask, but his eyes have that hard look that men's eyes get when they're facing off with one another. Even though neither one of them is moving, I get the sense that's exactly what's happening. I'm not even sure I understand why.

"This doesn't concern you," Grayson says.

"I'm not so sure about that," Jack says in a hard voice.

"Just go," I say miserably, looking at Grayson, then away to the darkened windows. The horrible scene is reflected back at me. I see Jack's face plainly. His body is framed by the open door.

In the window's reflection, I catch a glimpse of Grayson's profile as he glances at me, then back at Jack. He doesn't move. His stance has not relaxed at all.

"Please," I say. This is just making everything worse. "Just go."

In the glass, I see Grayson look at me. He keeps looking at me, but I won't return his gaze. I don't move. There's no undoing this.

He exhales sharply then heads for the door. Jack takes one step to the side, blocking Grayson's path. Grayson straightens, not intimidated. God, the last thing I need is these two going at each other.

"Jack," I say.

He looks at me, then catches my eye in the window. He's never looked at me like that before, with such sternness.

A heartbeat goes by and, still holding my eye, Jack steps aside and Grayson storms past.

I drop my eyes to my lap, but don't move. Jack doesn't move either.

"What the hell was going on?"

I hear the condemnation in his voice. It's the same contempt I feel for myself.

"You don't understand, Jack."

"No," he says quietly. "I don't."

"I'll tell Sam," I say dully, "but after the wedding. For Isabella's sake."

He doesn't respond to this.

I don't hear him go, but I sense it. Minutes later I look up. The doorway behind me is empty and I'm alone in a strange room, looking at a reflection of myself I don't recognize.

Chapter 16

I locate Ashley by the bar, getting a refill on her champagne. I walk up to her and, without a word, grab her wrist and drag her away toward the hall.

"What's going on?" she asks.

"Hang on." I'm not slowing and still hanging on to her wrist. We go into the same room I just left and I close the door behind us. Before she can say a word I tell her everything, hardly stopping for a breath. When I tell her how Grayson and I kissed, her eyes grow wide. When I tell her Jack caught us, her mouth drops.

That's still how she's still looking at me when I finish my story and lean back against the wall in exhaustion. She finally closes her mouth, but continues to stare at me. "I'm going to tell Sam," I say dully, "but not until after the wedding."

Ashley blinks. "Tell her... what exactly?"

"Everything." I know have to come clean, all the way. I'm going to tell Sam I'm in love with Grayson and then... all I can do is hope to God I didn't just lose one of my best friends. But I'm definitely <u>not</u> going to unleash all this right now and risk upsetting Isabella. The last thing anyone needs is Sam going nuclear on me in the middle of the celebrations. That means I still have two more days to get through somehow.

Fuck. What a week.

"Will you do me a favor?" I ask.

Ashley's eyes are still wide. She nods mutely.

"Will you please tell Grayson I can't talk to him until after the reception? I don't trust myself around him and I <u>definitely </u>don't want to be alone with him again until I've talked to Sam."

"Um. Okay."

I exhale, walk heavily to the Bed of Betrayal, and plop onto it. God, I'm a horrible, horrible person. I never knew what a horrible person I am.

Ashley watches me in silence, then says, "Are you guys... together now?"

"I..." I don't know. Part of me feels like we are, but we didn't exactly have a chance to discuss it. But if there's any question, I'll do everything I can to make it happen.

In two days.

I close my eyes with dread. In two days I'll likely be finding out if I still have a friendship with Sam or not. After betraying her like this, I can only imagine the shit storm that's coming my way. I've seen it with Sam before, but I've never been the target of it.

The truth is, I'll take every ounce she gives me if she'll only forgive me at the end of it. But will she?

As for Grayson, I don't know what he's going through right now and wish to God I could talk to him about it. But I don't intend on losing him again. Not if I can help it.

"I hope so," I finally answer Ashley. "I'll have to wait to find out."

I don't ask what she thinks Sam will say. She doesn't ask me either. We linger there in quiet acknowledgement of one simple fact:

no matter what happens next, this is one, big, fucking disaster.

The next morning, while I'm still in my room getting ready, I get a text from Jack.

Jack: Ashley talked to me.

Great.

Me: Okay.

I look in the mirror. The wedding isn't until tomorrow, but pictures are this morning. I'm in my bridal dress—a gorgeous teal strapless number with a knee-length, flowing skirt—and am putting the final touches on my makeup. My appointment with the resort's hair stylist is in fifteen minutes. I'm not sure what the rest of the guests are doing today, but between pictures, the rehearsal, and the rehearsal dinner, my day is pretty much spoken for. I don't expect I'll see much of Grayson, and that's a good thing.

Sort of. I miss him horribly. Traitorous person that I am.

Jack: Do you love him?

Me: Yes.

Jack never responds. I don't even know what to think about that.

I honestly don't know what to think about anything.

We're on the grand balcony at the resort, where the wedding will be held at three o'clock tomorrow afternoon. The stone balcony holds two hundred people, with the capability of completely opening the rear to allow for overflow for another four hundred in the interior room. It's an elegant, beautiful space facing the sea and will be, as I understand it, completely packed for the ceremony tomorrow.

At the front, the elaborate platform and arch under which Isabella and Shane will be married is already decorated with vines, flowers, and twinkle lights. We've already taken the group picture with the bridal party, as well as the group picture with the bridal party and all the immediate family.

We're currently scattered about the balcony in small groups, chatting and waiting to be called up by the photographer. He's taking pictures with the happy couple and their parents. Isabella is positively radiant. Her happiness is a welcome distraction from my own selfish worries.

As for Sam, I've kind of been soaking up this time with my friend. You know, just in case...

She, Ashley, and I are sitting near the rear of the balcony, out of the sun.

"What do you think about Shane's best man?" Sam asks calmly.

We both look across the way to where the best man is hanging out with the other groomsmen.

"He's kinda cute," Sam says, "right?"

"Not interested," I say.

"Not for you. For me."

Ashley and I both look at her with wide eyes. She glances at us and shrugs. "I think the thing with Grayson has run its course.

Not that I ever got in a full run in to start with."

Ashley glances at me—I'm just trying to make my face look normal—and asks, "What do you mean?"

Sam sighs. "We had an interesting talk last night. It kind of explained a lot."

My heart is pounding and I'm terrified Grayson's already told her everything. But part of me knows if she knew she wouldn't be sitting here calmly like this, instead of getting ready to claw my eyes out.

"What's going on?" Ashley presses.

"Well, I've been a little frustrated with him because..."

Ashley and I exchange nervous glances.

"Well... we haven't exactly had the roaring good time I was hoping for."

We both furrow our brows at her.

She rolls her eyes. "We haven't had sex," she clarifies.

"What?!" Ashley and I exclaim together.

"Shh!" Sam glances around. "It's not exactly something I want to advertise. I have my reputation to think about."

My head's spinning, but I'm not thinking about Sam's reputation.

"Wait," Ashley says. "You've been... sharing the same room right? And how long did you know him before, again?"

Sam shrugs. "Not that long. The way I picked him up was kind of funny, actually. We made out and stuff when we first met, but I wasn't that worried that it didn't go further because we just went out once and only texted in between. I figured once we got here it'd be different. But... it's been so fucking <u>weird</u> with him ever since we got here."

Ashley and I are holding each other's gaze. He didn't sleep with Sam. Oh God, he didn't sleep with Sam. I want to laugh with relief, but my mortification at the entire situation I'm in successfully prevents it.

"How did you guys share a bed and not sleep together?" Ashley asks. She seems kinda disbelieving, and knowing Sam the way I do, I'd probably be disbelieving too if I weren't so fucking happy my Sam has never had sex with my Grayson.

Sam raises a hand dismissively. "I don't want to lay out all the details. Let's just say I'm not going to force myself on someone who's not interested, I don't care how hot he is. Not that I haven't pulled out every trick in the book. Seducing someone is fair game, as far as I'm concerned."

Okay, I don't think I want to hear all this.

"I was..." Sam stops and gets a slightly pained look on her face.

"What?" I ask, concerned.

"I was kinda feeling bad. Like, maybe I'd lost my touch. I've never really had to worry about this before. I think I'm pretty good at screening people to start with. I know how to find guys who are willing... I just couldn't figure out where I got my signals mixed up. I mean, if he's the kind of guy who likes to wait, that's fine by me, but then what was he doing agreeing to share a hotel room with me for five nights, you know? What did he think was going to happen? It was kinda freaking me out. And I was none too happy about joining Chloe in the 'I desperately need a screaming orgasm' club, I can tell you that right now. He was just so hot and cold about things, you know? I couldn't figure it out."

Sam shrugs then. "He finally explained it all last night, though. Apparently, he's in love with some girl and he thought he was over her but he's not."

I look at Ashley urgently.

"So at least I know it's not me," Sam continues. "But, I gotta say, I would've liked him to figure out he was still hung up on this girl a little later because Grayson's fucking hot and unless I'm wrong, he would've been awesome in the sack."

God, Sam.

"He was actually really sweet about the whole thing once he finally came out with it, though. I couldn't really be too irritated."

"But a little irritated?" Ashley asks.

"Well, not with him. He's a good guy. But yeah I was hoping for more action this week, that's for damned sure. He offered to go home last night but I decided I didn't want him to. I mean, we cleared each other to, you know, pursue other options. But I'd rather not throw a kink in things for Isabella. He'll come to the dinner tonight since it's assigned seating. I don't want her worrying if no one's next to me or feeling like she has to shuffle things around or whatever. It's not a big deal. But he'll go home after that."

"You don't mind him being there?" Ashley asks.

Sam shrugs. "Nah. He's cool. It's not like there's any hard feelings. I don't mind if he comes, and he's willing to go along with it. I think he feels he owes me a favor. Anyway, now that I don't have to worry about trying to seduce him, I think we'll get along fine." Sam gets a devilish grin on her face. "I told him he was totally missing out, though."

I blink. I'm trying to wrap my head around the idea of Grayson and Sam joking around about the fact that they're not sleeping together.

"So he's not coming to the reception?" I ask.

Ashley mouths at me, "Tell her." I give a subtle but firm head shake <u>no.</u>

"I don't think he needs to," Sam answers, "and why would he want to? I'd rather he not be there anyway. It'll be easier to kinda do my thing, you know? I doubt Isabella will notice his absence and if she does I won't mind telling her at that point. I just don't want her worrying about me before then. It's really fine. Honestly, I'm glad it's over. I've had my eye on a few people since I've been here and since <u>Chloe</u> won't take any of them..."

<u>Wanna trade?</u> I think, but I keep my mouth shut.

God, if only I hadn't kissed Grayson last night. I could totally fess up right now. But what is she going to think when she finds out I kissed him behind her back like that?

"Maid of Honor!" the photographer calls out. Shane and the parents are exiting the platform, leaving just Isabella. "Then all the bridesmaids."

Sam turns to me. "How's my hair?"

I tend to a lock of curls that's starting to fray, feeling a confusing mix of guilt and hope and fear. She might be okay that things are done with Grayson—an eventuality we all knew was coming anyway—but there's still a big piece to this puzzle she doesn't know about and I'm terrified to see her reaction when she does.

I watch Sam approach Isabella, feeling I've betrayed all of us, in the end.

"I'm such a horrible friend," I say to Ashley.

She looks pained. "Maybe I gave you bad advice. Maybe I should have told you to tell her from the start."

"God, Ashley, none of this is <u>your</u> fault."

No. It's all on me.

I look at Isabella and Sam, both looking radiant and smiling for the camera.

It helps to know Sam and Grayson haven't slept together, and to hear it out of her own mouth that she's done with him. It does. But none of that changes the fact that I didn't know any of that when I started making out with Sam's date.

There's just no getting around the fact that I betrayed her, and Sam's going to know it.

I think back to the moment Sam found out Loni slept with Sam's ex. She hadn't cared about that guy either. It was the betrayal Sam couldn't stomach. I remember how she got that hard expression on her face, tore Loni a new one, told her to take a hike, and never looked back.

For all I know, I'm only two days away from the same fate.

After another hour of pictures, a break for lunch, and a repeat of the whole scenario so Isabella and Shane could have more pictures at the beach, I'm pretty exhausted. I change out of my dress and into more comfortable clothes for the rehearsal. By the time that's all over, we and the rest of the guests are gathering in one of the hotel's dining halls for the rehearsal dinner.

The food is incredible and there's even dancing. I wonder what they have in store for the reception if they're doing all this just for the rehearsal dinner. I stick close to Ashley, who's doing a good job keeping me away from Grayson. I need the backup too, because I'm having a hard time not going to him. Our eyes have met more than once, but

I try not to linger. It's too hard if I do. I really don't trust myself right now.

Jack's date arrived this afternoon, apparently, so she's keeping him occupied. I've barely spoken to him all evening. I'm surprised when, well into the evening's dancing, he approaches my table during a slow song and quietly asks me to dance.

I look up at him. He's neither smiling, nor scowling. He's simply looking at me and holding out his hand. With no small amount of trepidation, I take it. Heart pounding, I allow him to lead me onto the dance floor. I catch Grayson watching us just before Jack stops, pulls me into his arms, and starts to dance.

I don't say a word. Neither does Jack. He slowly pulls me closer, until we're holding each other tight. Fighting tears now, I rest my head against his chest.

"I'm sorry," I whisper.

After a moment, he says, "I know."

"I didn't mean to."

He sighs, but doesn't respond.

"Have you told Sam?" I ask.

"Why would I do that?" he asks quietly.

I don't know. We may joke about who Jack's favorite is, but we all know it's Sam.

When I don't reply he says, "You said you're going to tell her, right?"

I nod against his chest.

"Okay, then."

We go through the rest of the dance in silence. When it's over, he holds me by the shoulders and looks at me. "You tell her all of it," he says. "The whole story with you two. Okay?"

I don't answer and he doesn't wait for me to. He hooks my hand around his arm, escorts me back to the table, thanks me for the dance, and returns to his date.

At that point, I think I've had about all I can handle for the evening.

"I'm going to bed," I say to Ashley. "See you tomorrow."

"Okay, honey." She gives me a hug. "I think it'll be okay."

Uh-huh.

"We'll find out," I say, giving her a small smile.

I'm halfway down the hall, when I hear my name.

I spin and sure enough, there he is, coming toward me. I want to run to him and throw my arms around him and stay there for the rest of my life. What I <u>should</u> do is tell him to keep his distance and walk away myself. Instead I stand there, torn, until he's nearly to me.

"Wait." I raise my hand and glance at the empty hallway behind him. "We can't. Not until I talk to Sam."

"Can't what?" He's wearing a pained expression again. "What are we doing, Chloe?"

I look toward the open doors to the dining hall, the music pouring out. It's still empty, but that could change at any minute.

He looks behind him too, then takes me by both arms and steers me around a corner.

"We can't," I say, retreating farther down this second hallway, with him following me.

"I'm not trying to do anything with you. I just need to talk to you. Please."

I stop and face him. "I really don't trust myself around you."

He blinks at me. "What does that mean? Are you leaving again?"

"Am I—what?"

"Are you done?"

"Done with you? God, Grayson, no." I put my hands on his chest. His face relaxes a bit, but he still looks anxious. "No," I say again firmly. "I just... it's bad enough kissing you once behind Sam's back. I really, really don't want to do that again. I'm going to talk to her, but not until after the wedding. I don't want to risk upsetting Isabella."

He takes a deep breath. "Alright."

He looks like he wants to kiss me though. This close to him, taking in his smell, I'm having a really, really hard time resisting him too.

I already kissed him once, a traitorous voice inside me says, What difference will one more make?

"Alright," he says again. "I'll wait."

I nod.

Okay. There it is. We've both agreed.

But, intending to be good or not, we're both leaning closer and closer to one another. I'm trying not to, I really am. But my hands grip the front of his shirt as my mouth tilts toward his.

"Only one," I whisper, just before our lips meet.

"Only one," he agrees, then his mouth is on mine and I exhale with relief. Oh how I've longed for his touch all day.

It's a short kiss, but it's all I need. It's enough to get me through.

We pull away and I don't linger. I turn and continue down the hall, feeling his eyes on me the entire way.

Chapter 17

The wedding day is here at last. It's been busy with preparations and yet more hair appointments. We're less than thirty minutes away from the ceremony. Sam, Ashley, and I are in a dressing room, watching Sam put the final touches on her makeup. Sam's been busy helping Isabella, who's in another room with her mother and grandmother, so while we've been ready for a bit, she's just now getting there.

As we sit here, though, I'm starting to realize how quiet Sam's been. We've been so busy, I hadn't really noticed it. She's sitting at a vanity, applying her blush, not saying a word.

"You okay, Sam?" I ask.

"Yes."

Though her answer is short, she doesn't sound mad or anything. She dips her brush into the compact and starts on the other cheek.

Ashley and I exchange glances. Ashley kind of shrugs. Maybe Sam's just distracted. She has been busy today.

"I can't believe Isabella's getting married," Ashley says.

"Isabella Brooks," I say. "That'll take some getting used to."

Suddenly, Sam turns toward me, tears brimming in her eyes.

I blink at her in surprise.

"How could you?" she whispers.

Instantly it's clear: Sam knows.

All my dread about her finding out drops over me in a split second. My skin is cold with fear.

"Sam, I—"

"You're supposed to be my friend." A crocodile tear escapes her lashes and runs down her cheek. She instantly turns away from me and yanks a tissue from the box, dabbing her eyes. She's being careful not to ruin her makeup. Her face is becoming a mask, as she focuses on what she's doing.

"I saw you two," she says flatly, still tending to her eyes. "In the hall last night."

God, I'm a stupid idiot. And a rotten friend. And there's no point denying any of that.

I no longer want to explain. I don't want to say I'd met Grayson before or that I love him. Because none of it really changes what I've done.

"Sam, please, I'm so sorry."

"So am I."

I glance at Ashley helplessly. She looks tortured. "Sam, you should know—"

"No," I say.

Ashley looks at me. "But..."

"No. It doesn't matter." I don't want it to sound like an excuse. Whether I was with Grayson first or not is irrelevant. I kissed him—twice—while he was here with Sam and she has every right to be hurt about that. I'm hurt about it myself.

Sam spins on Ashley. "You knew about this too?"

Ashley gapes at her, speechless.

Sam turns back to the mirror, angry and fighting tears.

<u>Oh God,</u> I think. "No, this isn't Ashley's fault."

"You need to tell her," Ashley says forcefully.

"It's no excuse."

Sam spins around to face me, arms crossed. "Tell me what?"

For a moment I'm frozen, caught in Sam's glare. But she's waiting, and I realize I have to say <u>something</u>.

I slowly approach and go down on my knees, looking up at Sam. She looks temporarily disarmed by this, but frowns at me, as if raising her defenses.

"I met Grayson before," I say quietly. "He's the one I was with the night I was supposed to marry Brad." Sam's eyes sharpen slightly, but otherwise her expression doesn't change and she does not move. "I'm so sorry I didn't tell you right away. I should have. I didn't know what to do. I thought..." my voice breaks, but I take a resolute breath and push on. I just need to get it all out.

"I fell in love with him that night and I know that sounds stupid but I did. It freaked me out so I ran out on him. I didn't see him again until he came here to be with you. I thought it was over anyway and I didn't want to ruin your week so I just—" I stop. Her expression still hasn't changed. "I should have told you. But I..."

"You're the girl?" Sam says. I don't know which I hear in her voice more, hurt or anger.

I nod helplessly.

"Why the fuck didn't you tell me?" she says sharply. "I was talking about it right in front of you and you said nothing."

I pinch my eyes closed briefly. "I know, I'm sorry. I didn't know how you were going to react and I didn't want to risk spoiling Isabella's wedding. I was going to tell you afterward."

Looking at her is too much for me. I'm a horrible friend and a coward, because the only way I can get through the next part is to look down at my hands clasped on my lap.

"I kissed him Thursday on the ship and I kissed him in the hall yesterday and I didn't mean to betray you. I swear to God, Sam, I didn't. But I know I did. And if I could go back and change everything I would."

I look back up at her. She still has the same hard expression. She's still frowning at me. But now her eyes are filled with tears. "I'm so, so sorry. God, Sam. I'm so sorry."

I can't even ask her to forgive me. Why should she?

As if in slow motion, Sam raises to her feet.

"I'm going to go help Isabella," she says flatly. "She doesn't need to know any of this right now. I'm not going to ruin my friend's wedding."

Then, I realize just how bad this is. Sam doesn't call me names or rage or even tell me to piss off. I've hurt her so much we're far, far past the nuclear stage. Because calm as you please, Sam leaves the room and closes the door quietly behind her.

Chapter 18

The ceremony is a little surreal.

Sam, Ashley, and I go through the motions pretty believably, I think. Sam smiles at Isabella like she couldn't be happier. I smile, too. It <u>is</u> a beautiful ceremony, made even more beautiful by our friend. Isabella's in a stunning custom-made dress, with a flared trumpet silhouette cut. The entire dress is covered in delicate lace, has Swarovski crystals adorning the bodice and train, and an open back showing her gorgeous, dark, Mediterranean skin. Shane is dashing in his black tux, and the tender look of love he gives Isabella when she comes down the aisle probably makes every woman present swoon.

I couldn't say, myself. Inside I feel nothing. I'm numb and feel like I'm watching the whole thing unfold without really being part of it.

Like I'm already on the outs.

Surrounded by the most perfect weather anyone could ask for, with a gorgeous view of the ocean, everything goes off without a hitch. At the conclusion of the ceremony, we all file into the Grand Ballroom for the reception. It's like something out of a fairy tale. There are flowers and lights everywhere, and a false ceiling made of graceful bands of silk. The tables are set with fine china, crystal goblets, and delicate silver flatware. There's not one, but two ice sculptures, and a string quartet playing at the far end.

We stand in the receiving line as people come through to give their well wishes and make their way to the tables. Ashley is standing between me and Sam in the line. Sam hasn't looked at me once.

Eventually we all join Isabella and Shane at the bridal table at the front and an army of waiters and waitresses proceeds to serve us a four-course dinner. I feel like I'm being swept along by the tide. I hear the dinner is excellent, but I wouldn't know. I'm eating dutifully, but I can't really taste it.

At last the meal is over, the quartet packs up, and the DJ takes over. Isabella and Shane head to the open floor in the center to have their first dance. When they're finished, the tide that's swept me along so far will be over. There will be no more obligations.

Then I'll be able to talk to Sam, if she'll hear me.

When the dance is over and the DJ invites the rest of us to join in, I turn toward Sam, two seats down from me.

But she's gone.

Thirty minutes goes by and Sam doesn't come back. That's when I go looking. I find her out in the hall, alone. She's sitting on a padded bench, leaning against the wall and chewing on her thumbnail.

I approach tentatively. Half way there, she notices me. I stop. She looks at me and drops her hand to her lap, saying nothing. I continue on until I'm to her, but I don't sit down.

She looks forward, still not talking. She looks so resigned and defeated. I would much rather she rage and tell me she hates me than see her like this.

"You can yell at me if you want," I say.

She looks at me and furrows her brow.

"Or call me names?" I suggest.

She rolls her eyes and looks forward again. "Sit down, Chloe."

I slowly lower myself to the edge of the bench.

"Have you told me everything? You know... everything?"

I'm not sure she really wants to know everything, or that I want to tell her. Haven't I said enough? "I don't want to give you excuses."

"Yes, yes." She rolls her eyes again. "But this isn't about you, okay? It's about me. Have you told me everything about you two or not?"

I press my lips together and hold my breath a moment. "No," I say quietly.

"Well then."

Now I remember what Jack said. He said I should tell Sam the whole story. And Sam is, after all, asking.

So I comply.

I tell the entire thing, leaving nothing out. I tell my story the way I told it to Ashley. The way I would tell my friend. After a while, Sam watches me, but her impassive expression doesn't change.

When I'm finished, she faces forward again and sits there for a while.

"I'm so, so sorry, Sam. Please believe me."

She looks at me then. "Thank you for explaining," she says quietly, then gets up and walks down the hall without another word.

Eventually I go back into the ballroom. I don't know if Sam is in here or not. I don't look for her. I find a table on the edge of the room—inhabited by elderly guests who seem perfectly content to watch the younger ones out on the dance floor—and park myself there.

The song the DJ is playing is a raucous one, and the dance floor is hopping. Isabella and Shane are really getting into it. Turns out, the professor knows how to move.

I couldn't say how long I sat there before I see Sam marching across the room, heading straight for me. I sit up straighter.

Oh God, here it comes. She's gonna go crazy on me right here and now. I've been wishing she were mad instead of so hurt she can barely talk, but now that my friend is apparently descending on me in all her nuclear glory, I'm as terrified as any sane person would be.

I stand as she gets closer, take half a step back, and flinch when she grabs my hand. But she's not wailing on me. She's leading me across the room.

"Uh, Sam?"

"Wait for it."

Maybe she's taking me where there won't be any witnesses. Somewhere she can hide the body?

We weave through the crowd and exit the ballroom. "Sam?"

She doesn't slow. She takes me straight to—

"Grayson?" I breathe.

He's standing in the hall and he's... smiling?

Sam and I halt directly in front of him. She grabs Grayson's arm, then puts my hand in his.

"There," she says.

I can only gape at her.

"You owe me fucking <u>huge</u>," Sam says.

I blink.

With a perfectly straight face, she gives me a wink and starts to walk away. "I swear. The trouble I have to go through just to get you a date for the reception."

Still stunned, I look at Grayson. He's giving me a tentative smile. "Can I have this dance?"

"I—" I hold up one finger. "Hang on."

I spin and hurry after Sam, launching myself and giving her a huge hug from behind.

"Oof! Get off me, woman!"

"Thank you, thank you, thank you," I say, still hanging on to her.

"Okay, okay." She disentangles herself and turns toward me.

She's giving me a sort of, "What am I going to do with you?" look.

"Do you forgive me? Really, truly?"

She rolls her eyes. "Okay missy, let's just get it all out, shall we?"

I clasp my hands together and nod, looking at her meekly.

"Yeah, I was hurt. Obviously, okay? I mean, what a dumb ass move."

I nod my head vigorously. Captain Dumb Ass. That's me.

"But there's one thing that got me more than anything else. Why didn't you just tell me from the beginning?"

I raise my hands helplessly. "I don't know. Because I'm a stupid idiot? I probably should have told you. But once I realized that, I thought it was too late to change it, and then he kind of, you know, became your property and—"

She raises her eyebrows incredulously. "Say what?"

"Well, because I didn't tell you. That kind of made him yours. Doesn't that make sense?"

"Fuck no," Sam says, but she doesn't look upset. "You could've just explained."

"I know. I should have. I was just... so afraid of losing you as a friend. And then I started thinking about what happened with Loni."

"Loni? Who the hell's..." Sam halts, then gets a dawning look on her face. "Oh that girl?" She rolls her eyes again. "God, Chloe, did you really think you mean so little to me? I wasn't as close to Loni as I am to you. That lunatic kinda drove me nuts anyway."

"I'm so sorry."

Sam sighs. "Just... stop saying you're sorry. I know you're sorry."

"I really am."

She gives me a sharp look. "I am going to smack you, woman."

I press my lips together.

Her expression softens and she sighs. "You love him, right?"

I nod.

"Are you sure?" she asks, her brows furrowed. "You know, I can't guarantee his effectiveness in the sack."

I snort and give a tentative half grin.

"Can't hold his liquor either." Sam's starting to grin herself. "And his idea of fun is to strap himself to this teeny, tiny rope and go careening down a mountain like a crazy person. Oh, hell, what am I saying? You two nut jobs are probably perfect for each other."

I smile and throw my arms around her. "Thank you, Sam."

I expect her to call me a lunatic and tell me to get off, but she doesn't. She squeezes me back.

Chapter 19

When I go back to Grayson, I have so many questions. So many things I want to say. I don't say any of it. I just launch myself into his arms and we grip each other tightly. Being in his arms, I feel my entire soul sighing with relief.

He squeezes me tighter and lifts me onto my tiptoes.

"I missed you so much," I breathe into his neck.

"Since yesterday or since nine months ago?"

"Yes."

He loosens his grip enough to kiss me. We open to each other and kiss deeply. Again, my soul sighs, satisfied. But the rest of me is just getting started.

"We have to go in there," he says lowly.

I nod, rubbing one hand up his chest. "Okay." I kiss him again, and this time he takes me with more hunger, cupping my face with one hand. I kiss him eagerly, my body lighting up.

He pulls back, still holding my face, his eyes smoldering. "I've been instructed to make sure you dance tonight."

"Okay." I return to his mouth. I don't want to know if Sam gave him any other instructions about what to do with me tonight. Besides, I have my own ideas.

As our tongues search each other, I press myself firmly against him. I feel him growing against me. It's all I can do not to wrap a leg around him right now.

Maybe a more reasonable person would wait until later, but, yeah. I'm totally not waiting.

I'm about to suggest we take a detour to my room when he's suddenly steering me backwards, still kissing me. He pulls away briefly, quickly checks the hall—still empty thank God, since we apparently have <u>no brains</u>—and opens a door behind me.

We slip into a small, dark conference room and he backs me against a wall. What little restraint we were exercising in the hall is completely gone now. Frantically kissing each other and breathing hard, I undo his belt buckle and zipper while he shimmies up my dress and slides off my panties. The second we're both exposed, he hooks his hands under my shoulders and lifts me easily.

Throbbing and ready, I wrap my legs around his waist. I gasp as he presses me against the wall and enters my wet channel in one smooth move.

Oh my God, how I've needed this man.

He thrusts into me eagerly and I allow a moan of pleasure to escape before remembering where we are and biting back further sounds. The bass of the music in the ballroom resonates through the wall. Gripping his shoulders, I arch my head back as he takes me again and again. "Grayson," I whisper. "God, yes."

As my slick channel tightens around his hard shaft, I feel every ridge of him rubbing against me. I tuck into his neck, and he tucks into mine. The sound and feel of our hot breaths surround me.

"Chloe," he says thickly.

"Yes," I breathe, clutching him tightly as he rides me hard. As the hot ecstasy pulsing in my clit starts to flow outward, bathing me in pleasure, I clamp even harder around his cock.

"God, Chloe."

"Take me," I whisper. My chest is flushing hot as his movements intensify. I try to bite back a cry, but it escapes as a desperate whimper. He pushes me high and hard. The pleasure in my body spikes and I throw my head back.

I'm about to come and his cock is so hard that I know he is too. He thrusts me furiously and I almost go over. I claw at his back as he thrusts me again, and I damn near come undone as my orgasm explodes at last.

I arch back, practically climbing up the wall. He comes too and the contractions of his climax press against mine and amplifies the waves of pleasure tearing through me.

"Grayson," I gasp. My body contracts with pleasure and I bite the fabric of his shirt in an effort not to cry out.

At last I'm released from the peak and waves of pleasure slowly bring me down to the tingling conclusion. He slows too, and we're left still and panting against the conference room wall.

He presses against me gently, his hands supporting me as my body starts to relax and my legs lose their strength. He keeps us there, his cock still inside me, as I release into his arms.

He's still tucked into me, but kisses me gently on the neck. Little ripples of pleasure dance away from the place his lips touch me.

"I..." he says kissing me softly again, "am so..." he lifts up and kisses me on the temple, "in love with you."

I look at him and he holds me firmly, keeping me safe and secure right where I am. He smiles and I smile back.

"I love you, too," I say. "So much."

His smile widens.

I'm starting to be aware of the fact that we're in a rather compromising position in an unlocked room and start to lower my legs. He gently slides out of me, then carefully helps me get back on my own two feet. There's nothing graceful about the redressing and hair fussing that follows, but we can't stop grinning at each other and our little burst of passion feels impossibly romantic to me anyway.

Once we're put back together, but still in the darkened room, he pulls me into his arms.

"I think I'd better get you back in there before I get into trouble." He rubs his nose against mine.

"I'm ready." Now that I've settled things with Sam and quenched my need for Grayson, even if only for the moment, I do want to go celebrate with Isabella and my girls.

"We still have some things to discuss," he says quietly.

I nod. I haven't forgotten that I'll be on a flight to Boise in less than 24 hours. God, how I'm regretting that move just now.

"We'll do it after," he says, kissing me sweetly. "Maybe in your room, where we can have some privacy?"

"Can we go to your place?" I ask tentatively.

"You want to come to my place?"

I nod. "I want to sleep in your arms tonight. Is that alright?"

"Of course." He gently tucks a lock of hair behind my ear and squeezes me. "I'd love that, Chloe."

Then he gives me one, last, lingering kiss, and Grayson and I leave our little cocoon to rejoin the rest of the world.

At first it's a little weird, to be dancing with Grayson so openly when he's been here with Sam all week, but it doesn't seem to bother her at all. In fact, judging by the way she and one of the groomsmen dance during a slow song, I'd say Sam has landed on her feet just fine.

A few times during the fast songs, a large circle forms—including Isabella, us girls, Jack, and our dance partners—with everyone bopping around and laughing. I feel like I could soar up to the ceiling, I'm so light.

After one of the slow songs, Jack comes up to us and pins my feet on the ground a bit. After putting his arm around my shoulders and planting a kiss on the top of my head, he turns his attention to Grayson.

"Grayson," he says, a smile on his face but a serious tone in his voice. He extends his hand, and when Grayson shakes it Jack hangs on. "A word?"

My smile falters as I glance between the two of them. They're still gripping each other's hands and holding each other's eyes. "Uh—" I say.

"Sure," Grayson says calmly, "I think that's a good idea."

"Uh—" I say again but they turn away from me and head toward the ballroom doors.

I stand there frozen, not sure what to think. Sam and Ashley come up to me. Sam's watching Jack and Grayson depart as well.

"Don't worry," Sam says, smiling, "he's not going to kick his ass or anything."

I glance at her, then look back to the doors, where they've both just disappeared. "Are you sure?" Jack kind of had that big brother look I've seen in him before.

Sam shrugs easily. "Pretty sure."

I bolt forward, toward the doors, but she laughs and grabs my arm, stopping me. "I'm kidding, ding dong. He just wants to talk to him."

"O-kaay," Isabella's firm voice says behind us. We spin to find her examining us with crossed arms. "Are you guys going to tell me what's going on with Grayson, or what?"

"Uh..." Sam says.

We look at each other. Where to begin?

"There was a little mix up," Ashley jumps in. She gives us a questioning glance.

Sam and I look at each other and shrug. I guess now's as good a time as any.

Permission granted, Ashley proceeds to give Isabella the condensed version of events. Isabella's eyes widen almost immediately, then we watch as various expressions of astonishment cross her face. Sam and I are both trying to give her reassuring looks.

"So they got it all worked out," Ashley finally concludes. "It's okay."

"It really is," Sam says.

"Because Sam's awesome," I say.

"Fucking awesome," Sam agrees.

I have to smile, but Isabella's still giving us this look of disbelief. Poor thing. It's a lot to catch up on in just a couple of minutes. Maybe we should've waited.

"Really, it's—" Ashley starts, but Isabella holds up one hand, stopping her. Her mouth is partially open and her brows are furrowed.

We all hold our breath, watching her.

"Let me see if I've got this straight." She looks between me and Sam. "Out of the two of you," she points at me, "Chloe's the one getting laid tonight?"

My eyes fly wide and my mouth drops open.

A sly grin emerges on Isabella's face.

That little stinker!

Sam doesn't miss a beat. "Oh, I'm getting laid tonight, don't you worry about that."

She points through the crowd. "With <u>that</u> guy right over there."

With that, Sam heads in the direction of the lucky groomsman, glancing back over her shoulder and giving us a wink.

We watch her go, smiling, but Isabella gets serious again when she turns back to me and Ashley. "Is she really okay?"

Ashley nods. "I think so."

"And are <u>you</u> okay?" Isabella asks me.

"I am now, yes. I'm really, really glad it's over."

Isabella's aunt comes up and taps her on the shoulder. "You and your dad are up next."

Isabella glances over her shoulder. Her father is waiting for her on the edge of the dance floor.

"Okay, I'll be right there," she says, and her aunt leaves.

She looks back to me. "You'll fill me in later, right?"

I nod and give her a hug. "You look beautiful, Isabella. The wedding was perfect." I've said all this already, but it's nice to say it again when I'm not in such a fog.

"Thanks, Chloe," she says, beaming. She gives us both a smile before heading off to dance with her dad.

Ashley smiles at me. "I told you it would be okay."

"Because you never had any doubts," I say smiling.

"Nope. Not a one." We laugh, but then I see Jack and Grayson reemerge. They're both laughing.

I exhale heavily.

"See?" Ashley says. "No worries, honey." She pats me on the arm and goes back to the dance floor as I head toward Grayson. Jack gives me a wink, but spots his date and heads in that direction.

"What happened?" I ask, as I get close to Grayson.

He gives a little laugh. "I feel like I've just been interrogated by your father or something."

"What? Why? What did he say?" I'm starting to get worked up but Grayson takes my hand and squeezes.

"It's okay. Jack's a good guy. I think he just wanted to make sure I'm not the kind of guy to..."

He trails off and I furrow my brows. I know he's trying to reassure me, but I see the discomfort on his face. Whatever they discussed, it's left a mark.

"Well," Grayson continues, "after the way he found us he wanted to make sure..."

He trails off again, but I think I understand. "You're not the cheating type?"

Grayson nods and frowns. "You know, I realize Sam and I were never exclusive, but I also knew you and I shouldn't have been doing that. I'm not.... It's not one of my finer moments."

"No," I say seriously. "Me either."

"Does... stuff like that worry you?"

"That you'll turn out to be a cheater?"

"No. Well, I mean I don't want you to worry about that, because I'm really not that kind of guy."

"I know."

"No, I mean..." He sighs. "The whole point of the Rule was to avoid doing stupid things. And here it seems I've been making bad decisions all week long."

"Well," I kind of laugh and shrug. "I hate to tell you this, but people do stupid things when they're in love whether they're twenty-five or fifty-five. It just... can't be helped."

He laughs and pulls me into his arms. "That's not very reassuring." We begin to sway to the music.

"But if things work out, it's worth it." I give him a broad smile and raise my eyebrows. "Right?"

I have no idea what's going to happen next with us. I'm getting on a plane tomorrow afternoon and heading back to my job in Boise, whether I want to or not. But for now, Grayson's here, and I'm here in his arms, and that's a start. I'll take it.

He smiles and gives me a gentle kiss. "It's already worth it."

Chapter 20

It's almost three in the morning when Grayson and I walk into his kitchen and I'm back to where it all began.

Is it weird to say I feel like I'm coming home?

Holding my hand, he leads me into the living room, setting my suitcase at the foot of the stairs. The wall of windows, open to the city beyond, lets in enough moonlight for us to see by. We settle on the couch, facing one another, hands intertwined.

I let out a deep breath.

"Quite a day," he says quietly.

I raise my eyebrows and nod. "Uh, yeah."

"How tired are you? Would you rather talk in the morning?"

"I'm pretty tired," I acknowledge, "but I want to tell you what I'm thinking."

"What are you thinking?" He says this calmly, but I sense some nervousness underneath. I'm feeling a bit of nerves too, remembering what happened the last time I was here. But things are different now.

"I'm thinking a move back to Swan Pointe is in order."

He smiles. "I like the way you're thinking."

"You know don't you, that I'd be coming back for you. That's not too much for you, is it?" I do feel the need for both of us to be perfectly clear, but I confess, I'm not much worried about his answer at this point.

He raises one eyebrow. "You're kidding, right?"

I smile. "Kind of."

He rests his elbow on the back of the couch and leans his head on his hand. He rubs the back of my hand with his thumb. "I'm definitely not too happy about the idea of you being in Boise."

That makes two of us.

The company I work for will soon have one less cog working for them, but I have a feeling they'll manage just fine. It's fine by

261

me, too. I wish my blog were making enough to live off of, but I'm not there yet. "I don't know how quickly I can find a job here, but I'll start looking tomorrow. The sooner the better."

He opens his mouth, as if to say something, but seems to think better of it and closes it again.

I lean in and give him a gentle kiss, inhaling slowly. I pull away and put out my hand, palm up. "Phone please."

He furrows his brow at me, but pulls his phone out of his pocket and puts it in my hand. I bring up his contacts and start adding my information. "It's way past time for you to have my number." When I'm done entering my info into his phone and send myself a text so I have his number too, I set his phone on the cushion next to me. "I expect frequent calls and texts," I say smiling.

He's grinning too. "Can I take you to dinner on Friday? You know good places in Boise, right?"

I look at him in surprise.

"You're not the only one who can hop on a plane, you know."

"Oh," I breathe, "That sounds so heavenly!" I give him one kiss, which turns into half a dozen more enthusiastic kisses.

He laughs lowly. When I rest my head against the couch, smiling at him, he runs his hand through my hair. Part of me is so tired. I could fall asleep right here. The other part of me doesn't want to miss a second of Grayson. That's the part of me that wins. I haven't stopped smiling since he said he's coming to Boise.

Five more days. I'll get to see him again in five more days.

In some ways that feels like torture, but it's better than nothing. Who knows how soon before I can be back in Swan Pointe where I belong?

I sit here happily, watching him as he slowly runs his hand through my hair. He pauses just long enough to gently touch the tip of his finger to my nose piercing, like planting a little kiss on it. I smile sleepily.

"Smile for me," I say softly as he continues to play with my hair. He furrows his brow, but a crooked smile emerges. God, he's so damned cute.

I bring my fingertip to my lips, put a kiss on it, then place the tip of my finger on his dimple. He smiles deeper and catches my fingers before I can drop them. He puts my fingers on his lips so he can kiss them, then lowers my hand in his and gently rubs my hand with his thumb again.

My body betrays me, and I cover my mouth as I lose the fight not to yawn.

"Oh, big yawn," he says quietly, smiling. "Come on." He stands slowly and extends his hand to me. "Let's get you to bed."

I put my hand in his and go with him toward the stairs. He grabs my suitcase and we silently head up to the master bedroom.

I look at him and he gives me a gentle smile, his dimple just making an appearance. My heart flutters in response. I can imagine us doing this every night, for the rest of our lives.

Once upstairs, we go through a silent routine of sorts. We brush our teeth and get undressed. I drape my clothes over my suitcase, but don't bother retrieving my night slip. He's down to his boxers, but by the time I'm in only my bra and underwear, he's left off undressing and is standing still, watching me.

I'm feeling more awake now, I'll admit.

Eyes on his, I quietly remove my bra and slide it off my shoulders. As I'm exposed, his eyes slide downward, taking me in. Heart pounding, I let my bra drop to the floor.

Slowly, I hook my thumbs over the lacy band of my panties. He looks back up at me—with an impossibly loving expression that gets my insides dancing—then watches as I slide my panties down my legs. I let them fall to my ankles, then carefully step out of them, moving slightly in his direction.

He lets out a long, shaky exhale.

I stand still as he slowly comes up to me. He places his hands softly on my shoulders, then lightly trails them down my upper arms and over to my breasts. Goosebumps rise on my skin. His palms reach my erect nipples, and he cups me gently before continuing on to my stomach.

I raise my hands to his forearms. I rest them there lightly, then run my hands up to his firm biceps, and over to his chest.

His fingertips gently caress my belly button piercing. He leans in, placing his mouth on mine. I part my lips to receive him. My knees weaken as his tongue dances gracefully with mine. I take hold of him for support as his arms encircle my waist, bringing my naked flesh against his, linking us from chest to thigh.

Opening to a deeper, gentle kiss, I softly tug on the waistband of his boxer shorts. He pulls away quietly and slips them off. I stand, exposed and tingling and waiting, until he wraps his arms around me again.

Kissing me slowly, he continues to run his hands softly over my shoulders and back and rear. I'm lightly running my hand over his body as well, his hard desire for me gently pressing against the cleft of my sex.

He cups my face, intensifying his kiss. I tighten my hold on him, pressing harder against his firm chest. Still holding my face with one hand, he drops the other to my breast and squeezes gently as he starts working his mouth down my neck. I exhale a long breath as I tilt my head, giving him more room. My skin tingles everywhere his lips touch me.

As he continues to work down to the base of my neck, to my collar bone, and further down, he gently steers me to the bed until the mattress is against the back of my legs. I grip his shoulders firmly as he works his way down. My nipple is aching, but I wait for him. His hands lightly trail down the side of my torso until his mouth is hovering above my nipple. As he latches on, sending shivers over my body, he grips my hips tightly.

I let out a shaky exhale. What kind of sweet torture is this?

He gently sucks me, lightly trailing his hands over my ass and gripping my upper thighs from behind.

I let out a whimper and reach my hands down the length of his back.

He plants a trail of soft, hot kisses from one nipple and toward the other. I angle my hips and thighs closer to him, pressing against his body. He reaches my nipple, but doesn't suck it right away. He lightly flicks it with the tip of his tongue, teasing me.

I look down at him, my mouth slightly open, and slide my hand into his hair. He fully takes me into his mouth, tightening his arms around me as he sucks firmly.

I let out a soft moan. I'm throbbing and weak in the legs. But still I don't rush him. As he sucks my nipple, sometimes softly, sometimes firmly, I run my hands over his cheek and neck and shoulders. I've never given so much love in a single touch, or been loved so well in return.

He gives my nipple one last, firm taste, swings over and does the same to the other one, then comes up to my waiting mouth. Kissing me deeply, he gently adjusts me into a sitting position on the bed, his warm body between my thighs.

I don't know how much more of this I can take. I want to wrap my legs around him, but still I wait.

He pulls away, looking me deep in my eyes before slowly lowering his head and placing his lips on my breastbone. He works his way down, planting moist kisses in between my breasts and toward my stomach. My nipples are aching for his touch, but that isn't the only thing. As he gently lays me back, his mouth still wandering downward, I bring my knees up in anticipation of his ultimate destination. By the time he reaches the top of my pubic bone, I'm spread and lifting my hips up, unable to help myself. I'm throbbing and wet and I know it won't take me long to get there once he finally satisfies my need for his touch.

He continues downward, but veers to the side and gently sucks on the tendon at the top of my upper thigh. I grip his shoulder with one hand, his hair with the other. He goes over to the other side, his hot breath teasing my clit. I arch my back, enjoying the delicious frustration. He sucks on the other tendon, closer to the folds of my sex this time. I spread myself further and tug his hair in the desired direction, asking.

His head moves as directed and my clit throbs in expectation, a little heartbeat. "You're so beautiful, Chloe," he says softly, then laps his wet tongue over my clit. My mouth drops open and my body jolts as I'm consumed with the pleasure of him making contact at last. He licks and sucks and works me into a frenzy quickly. I moan and grind my hips toward his mouth helplessly. He slides two fingers into me.

I groan and press him hard against me, panting as I curl inward and spread my legs further. Intense waves of pleasure pulse outward from my clit, rising and rising as he licks me eagerly and fucks me with his fingers.

I urgently hang on to his shoulders as I climb to the pinnacle, my legs trembling. He flicks his tongue hard over me, thrusts me with now three fingers, and I let out a long, yearning cry as I'm shattered into a hundred glittering pieces.

I let out one sharp, short cry after another as he expertly leads me from one peak to the next, slowly bringing me down until I'm a limp, panting, puddle on his bed.

He gently removes his fingers and I'm left tingling and gazing at him with heavy eyes. He places a firm kiss on the middle of my inner thigh and I shiver slightly.

His gaze meets mine then and my heart skips a beat when I see the hot longing in his eyes. I don't know if I have strength enough to receive that longing, but I'm about to find out. Keeping his eyes on mine, he crawls up to me. I try to scoot up farther on the bed to give us a better base, but I'm too weak to do it very effectively. He effortlessly lifts me and moves me up. I raise my knees and he settles on top of me, his bulging cock hitting its mark.

One stroke inside my sensitive channel is all it takes. The fire is rising in me again. I exhale sharply as I grip his firm ass, squeezing him.

"Do you like that?" he asks huskily, rocking me firmly.

I nod, too weak to speak.

"How much do you like it?" I'm tightening around him.

"Don't stop," I whisper.

Supporting himself on his elbow, he grabs my hair and presses his forehead against mine. Still rocking me hard, he holds my eyes.

"You feel so good, baby. I missed you so much."

The pleasure in my body kicks into a higher place and I clamp even harder around him. He groans and closes his eyes, diving deep into me again and again.

"Look at me," I whisper.

His eyes flutter open, then close again in pleasure. He kisses me deeply, thrusting into me faster. I'm peaking higher as he penetrates me repeatedly. He lifts his head back just enough to lock his gaze with mine.

My entire body flushes hot and my heart is pounding out of my chest. His cock hardens even more as he continues to ride me and I see he's close. I'm close too and starting to tremble.

"I love you," I whisper as we move together, holding each other's eyes.

He grunts and closes his eyes briefly. Almost there, baby. I'm peaking right along with him.

He opens his eyes and I'm shuddering with barely contained pleasure. I whisper again, "I love you."

"I love you, Chloe," he says tightly, then contracts sharply over me as we both come together. He drops his weight fully on me and I shudder underneath him as he sends me into a place of pure bliss. When it's over, my legs drop heavily, too drained to do anything more. I weakly bring one hand to the back of his head and into his hair, lightly caressing him.

He comes up, cradles my face in one hand, and looks at me like I'm a pure wonder. Still panting softly, I give him a dopey smile. "How have I survived twenty-five years without you?" he asks.

I shrug, still smiling but too worn out to be much use. My eyelids are heavy. My whole body is heavy and warm and so, so happy.

He laughs lowly and gently rearranges us until I'm nestled in his arms, which are wrapped tightly around me.

I close my eyes and feel my body getting heavier.

"Sleepy, darling?" He gently kisses my forehead.

I nod my head slowly, my eyes still closed. His arms feel so good. He smells so amazing. I love him so much.

My eyes stay closed as he does a bit of reaching. I relax even more as he pulls the soft covers over our intertwined bodies. I slide into a warm, satisfying sleep.

The next morning, I'm pulled out of my cozy sleep when Grayson quietly gets out of the bed. I blink groggily at his back as he sneaks into the bathroom and closes the door silently. I indulge in a slow stretch, wishing I could stay in Grayson's bed forever.

Though, apparently, my bladder will have none of that. My stomach growls for good measure. I look at the clock on the nightstand: eleven o'clock. No wonder I'm starving.

I sigh. I have to leave for the airport in five and a half hours. Six maybe. I consider how long it might take me to get through security on a Sunday afternoon and wonder how far I can push it. Six and a half hours?

I hear the shower water turn on.

That's definitely not helping my bladder.

Still buoyant from another heavenly night of Grayson, I crawl out of bed and find another bathroom. When I'm finished I return to the bedroom, intending to crawl back into bed, but decide to make us breakfast instead. I don't know what he has in mind for that, but I'm too hungry to wait to find out.

I find my panties, slip on his button-down shirt, and pad barefoot down the stairs and into the kitchen. After acquainting myself with his pantry, I get started on some French toast.

I'm just laying the first pieces in the pan when I hear his voice upstairs.

"Chloe?"

My heart clenches instantly, responding to the faint hint of panic in his voice. God, how could I be so stupid? "I'm here!" I call quickly.

He appears on the landing, a navy blue towel wrapped around his waist. I see the relief on his face before he wipes it away, smiling at me.

"Are you making breakfast?" He starts coming down the stairs. God, he looks yummy. Maybe I'll just eat him up instead.

I meet him at the base of the stairs. "I figured I owe you."

He pulls me in firmly and gives me a kiss. "I thought you'd gone," he confesses quietly.

"I know, I'm sorry." I squeeze him. "I wasn't thinking."

"You know, I think you were right about this whole being in love thing," he says smiling.

"Right about what?"

"It makes you stupid."

I smile back, but as I think back to the Morning After the Night of Grayson, I grow more serious. His smile fades too, and he watches me, waiting. "You know," I say quietly, "when I left before, it was because I thought staying with you was the safe thing to do. I thought I'd be letting myself get caught up in a man. And, in a way, it would have been. Back then. I really did_need time to figure myself out and just be me. You know?"

He nods.

"But," I continue softly, "in some ways, <u>running away</u> was the safe thing to do. It was the easy way out. Staying with you, that would've been the risk."

"And you're feeling ready for that risk now?"

I nod.

"You're sure?"

I sigh. "I really, really, really don't want to get on that plane today."

He takes my face in his hands. "Then don't. Stay with me, Chloe. Today," he kisses me on the nose, "tomorrow," he kisses me on the forehead, "forever." He kisses me on the mouth.

I kiss him back, falling and falling and letting Grayson catch me. Because that's finally the one thing that makes sense.

We pull apart and I look into those stunning blue eyes. My Grayson.

Then I say out loud—and with my whole body and mind and soul—what my heart felt all those months ago.

"Yes," I say. "I'll stay."

The End

About the Author

Jordyn White writes steamy romances featuring smart, sexy women and the swoon-worthy men who adore them. Her sexy love stories are full of passion but don't skimp on the tenderness. She's addicted to trendy coffee houses, poolside lounging, and HEAs. When not tapping blissfully away on her laptop, she takes time to enjoy life with her husband and their children.

JordynWhiteBooks.com

CPSIA information can be obtained
at www.ICGtesting.com
Printed in the USA
BVHW030902290319
544056BV00002B/238/P

9 781945 261435